CUT OFF

Cut Off

 This book is a work of fiction. Names, characters, places, and incidents either are products of the author's imagination or are used fictitiously. Any resemblance to actual events or locales or persons, living or dead, is entirely coincidental. Violations may be subject to civil or criminal penalties.

Library of Congress Control Number: 2015949540

ISBN: 978-1-63308-170-3 Paperback
978-1-63308-172-7 Hardback
978-1-63308-171-0 Digital

Interior and Cover Design by R'tor John D. Maghuyop

1028 S Bishop Avenue, Dept. 178
Rolla, MO 65401

Printed in United States of America

JODI ELDER AND JAMI ENGELBRECHT

CUT OFF

CHALFANT ECKERT
PUBLISHING

ACKNOWLEDGEMENTS

We would like to thank all of our family and friends for their loyalty and love throughout our process of writing this book. Without our experiences with our students over the years, we would not have had the insight to share the trials and joys of being a teenager. Thank you as well to our husbands, daughters, mother, father, brothers, and grandparents. We would never have achieved this dream without your support and encouragement throughout the process. You all allowed us to gain independence, finding quiet, hiding places to dream as children..especially atop the sawdust pile. We love you all.

FRIDAY

The little boy cried despite my efforts to console him. His little, frail arm laid at his side clearly dislocated. Slumped against the seat in front of us, the boy's face was as pale as the descending snowflakes outside the bus window. I wanted to help him, but I was afraid to move him.

The injured boy's pained moans blended into the chorus of the other children around us, crying from their own injuries or from fear. Ironically, another eighth grader on the bus, Emily, was the only passenger who appeared to be calm. She moved up and down the bus aisle, from child to child, assessing injuries like an emergency room doctor.

Blood droplets dripped from one little girl's head like a fountain.

"You'll be fine, sweetheart," Emily whispered into the girl's ear in a tender, empathetic voice much unlike her everyday voice. Her voice was nearly unrecognizable, because it was so different than her normal voice at school.

"It's just a little scratch," Emily said, wiping the little girl's blood with her shirt. "Head injuries bleed worse than injuries sustained to other parts of the body. Thousands of blood vessels run back and forth across the skin's surface kind of like a jungle gym at the playground."

The little girl smiled at Emily, when she realized she wasn't hurt badly.

Emily continued talking to the little girl, as she cleaned and bandaged her wounds, "Heads bleed a lot more than other places, but you're going to be just fine. You just need to sit up straight, so the blood can flow right down to your toes. Do you feel dizzy or like you are going to fall asleep?"

The little girl, who I recalled was in my little brother Sammy's class and was named Annie, stopped crying and shook her head. Emily emptied the little girl's backpack onto the seat.

"Whatcha doin'?" Annie asked, blowing her nose into a tissue Emily gave her. "I don't think I'm gonna go to sleep. I was just a little scared, but I'm better now."

This time Emily didn't answer. She pulled a pair of scissors out of her coat pocket and cut the girl's cotton backpack into thin strips. Emily then stuck the scissors back down into her pant waist, like a makeshift tool belt, next to a pocket knife, a bottled water, a pencil, and a bottle of iodine. She then wrapped one of the thicker strips around little Laura's head and told her she'd be back in fifteen minutes to check on her. The little girl nodded and sat very stoically with the cotton bandage around her head.

Emily moved to the next seat on the bus and peered down at the child, prepared to take care of him. The little boy didn't look like he was very hurt at all.

"Emily, over here," I yelled, hoping she would skip him and move to this other little boy. I tried to yell loud enough so she'd hear me over the noise of kids crying. "This boy's really hurt."

Emily started in my direction. She looked surprised I called her by name. The sounds of children crying and the motor gurgling nearly made my ears ring.

Without warning or even a word, Emily walked over to the little boy, pulled him up out of his seat, and jerked his arm right back into its socket.

"What are you doing?" I asked Emily, when the little boy screamed.

She didn't answer, but the little boy grew quiet, just as quickly as he shrieked in pain.

"Sorry," I responded. "Apparently, you knew what you were doing."

"It's better to move quickly and without warning," Emily said. "Then the patient doesn't have time to think about treatment. Sometimes patients respond more dramatically because their expectations of pain outweigh the reality of their physical pain. The actual event is often less difficult than expected."

"I didn't realize you're a doctor," I said. My response wasn't meant to sound sarcastic. Emily had to know how grateful we all were that she took charge. "How do you know all of this?"

Emily was in one of my classes at Jefferson Junior High, so I knew she was super smart. She knew every answer to every question in class, and she was a little strange, but I had no idea someone our age knew so much about medical treatment.

Emily didn't answer me, but continued navigating her way up and down the aisle, examining the few passengers left on the bus and assessing their levels of injury. She tended to the kids with more serious injuries and afterwards moved on to minor injuries, without saying a word to anyone, except herself.

"Dr. Z says to start from the end and move to the beginning," she whispered to herself. "Examine and deliver. Examine and deliver."

An outsider wouldn't believe Emily was an eighth grade student, as she repeated instructions to herself. Who was this Dr. Z she mentioned? The name sounded vaguely familiar. Emily carried a small notebook and took notes after treating the passengers.

No one appeared to be too badly injured other than their bumps and bruises. The little boy moved his arm again. His name was Troy, I thought. He was one of the Smith boys who lived a few trailers away from me. I looked back out the bus window to see if anyone was coming down the hill to help us yet. Outside the window, a blinding white sheet of snow poured down outside so thick it was nearly impossible to see the patch of trees surrounding us.

Our driver, Mr. Mike, laid in the front next to his driver's seat at the base of the gear shift in a fetal position. Emily kneeled over him, and it looked like she was waking him up. The bus was warm, but cold air already began to seep through the cracks in the broken bus windows. I looked down again to see Sammy laid helplessly next to me. His head was covered in blood. I lost it.

WEDNESDAY

JETT

Weaving in and out of oblong tables, the smell of boiled cabbage mingled with boys' cologne. Either the nasty cafeteria food smell or my nervous stomach made me nauseous. I walked through our school cafeteria like a zombie. A teacher motioned for me to pull the stocking cap off my head. I reluctantly obeyed, revealing my haircut, and searched desperately for an empty seat. I wished I could disappear. My social status had dropped to "nobody."

Christmas break was way too short. Every day of the break I prayed my hair would grow back out, but even prenatal vitamins couldn't bring it back. Now the break from school was over, and we were back to the stresses of homework and attempts to impress each other. The farther I made it into the cafeteria, I was Alice, climbing through the looking glass, a mirror portal into another time and another place.

Although a plastic, olive green tray occupied my hands in real life, in my mind, I held my camera, taking pictures of this new wonderland. I walked throughout the crowded, loud room, ignoring the French fries flying by my head. This wonderland was colorful and fun much like my life before. That's how I viewed my days at school, pretending to watch the events through my camera lens. The snapshots recorded a different picture.

Last night, I dreamed when I returned to school, I was praised for my fashionable change and was appreciated for its dramatic flair. Upon seeing me Chloe threw her arms up to run her thin fingers through my short, trendy strands and exclaimed how amazingly gorgeous it made my eyes look. We stood in the hallway, talking about everyone who walked by and checking out each other's new Christmas outfits. We acted like we hated coming to school, but deep down we loved every minute of it. We were center stage, as all of the other kids watched our reunion with envy. Oh, how they wished they could be cool like us. Our rambunctious outpour of joy inflated our egos.

We performed the act to remind our less fortunate, unpopular classmates how happy we were in our perfect, little world. This reunion was our prime opportunity to put on a show for the unpopular kids, so they could see how good it was to be cool. The rest of the student population watched us, knowing they would never gain access to this level of popularity. Our world was so far from their reach, like a wardrobe into a secret world they'd never find.

The world of popularity belonged to the elite—those of us who seemed to have it all. This was the only world in which eighth grade students at Jefferson Junior High were truly happy. I knew this because I had been on both sides.

I awoke from my dream feeling a tiny bit of confidence. I got out of bed to use the restroom and faced a reflection that wasn't trendy, dramatic, or amazingly gorgeous. I decided to go back to bed to get one last hour of rest before I faced the harsh critics, which I once happily contributed.

What happened to me over Christmas break was horrible. I was hoping the aftermath at school wouldn't be as painful. On the first day back to school after the incident, the torment began. My best friend, Chloe, waited for me at the locker we shared, looking perfectly put together, as usual. She wore her auburn hair in a high bun piled on top of her head like Grace Kelly. Her knee-high leather boots demanded attention. She wore a matching leather duffel bag over her shoulder and flicked the point of a pen in and out as she waited for me to start our day.

"Hey," I hesitantly muttered, moving the combination lock in between numbers. "How was your weekend?"

If I pretended nothing had changed, then it would all be back to normal. I'd recited this chant a hundred times on the bus before unloading at Jefferson Junior High.

"Jett, what in the heck have you done?" she asked me. Her twinkling hazel eyes twitched back and forth between shock and humor.

"Is this a joke?" she asked, touching my hair to see if it was real. "Is that a wig? Take it off, Jett. It looks HORRIBLE."

"I...um...was ready for a change," I lied, pretending like my hair looked like it did before, long and gorgeously blonde. Chloe reacted just as I expected. I wanted so badly to open up and tell her what all I'd been through. I'd sworn not to. I knew it'd be a bad idea.

"Has Keagan seen *it*?" Chloe asked, now beginning to openly burst out in laughter.

The way she said *it* was like *it* was an evil troll dancing on my head.

"*It*'s even worse than I thought it would be," she said, shaking her head in disgust.

"What is that supposed to mean?" I asked. "No, Chloe, no one has seen *it*."

So much for being there for each other like best friends should.

"And it's really not funny," I said. "I didn't want it to look like this. I know it's horrible, but it's just hair. It'll grow out."

"Well, you've done quite a number," she finished, slamming her locker with one final look at my hair. "I don't think anything can fix *it*."

I thought about telling her what really happened, but the story was even more embarrassing than the hair on my head. That was the last thing she said to me before turning away. Our friendship was over just like that. At lunch, Chloe didn't wait for anxiously as usual to fill me in on all of the gossip. She hadn't said a word to me. I walked toward our regular table and hoped my friends encouraged me to sit with them. I hoped they'd give me some possible suggestions on how to cover up the hideous shag, until my regular hair grew out again.

Keagan, my boyfriend, and the rest of our friends sat at our normal table. After placing an apple and juice on my tray, I made my way in their direction. Food didn't sound good, even though my stomach growled. Eyes scanned me like a metal detector, as I walked by their tables. Muffled whispers and laughter followed me.

To them, I was a leper, and my unpopularity was contagious. With each step, my eyes filled up more and more, threatening to overflow at any second. I pushed back the tears with all I had in me.

"What in the heck did she do that for?"

"Well, if that ain't a dang shame," echoed from the cowboys' table.

I paused momentarily near the brainiac, overachievers' lunch table to search for an open seat and hoped someone would invite me to sit with them. Just like every other eighth grader in the cafeteria, the brainiacs enjoyed the challenge of coming up with new predictions as to my hair transformation.

One nerdo with a mullet told the other nerds, "She must have underestimated the chemical potential of Clairol coloring."

Another girl at the table commented, "With the average human hair only growing 1.25 centimeter or 0.5 inches per month, it will be at least 8,760 days before she ever resumes the length she previously wore."

I made eye contact with the girl, and she quickly looked back down at her tuna sandwich on wheat. The girl's name was Emily. She was in my Biology class and we rode the same bus.

Miss Know-It-All, Emily, lived in the new subdivision a few blocks from my trailer park and always settled her awkward body in the front seat of the bus. From my observations, she relished the thirty-minute drive to school, reading her book without being bothered. Once in a while, she popped off questions to our bus driver, Mr. Mike, who always patiently responded to her inquisition. Walking toward Emily and her brainiac friends, I knew they didn't plan to make room for me at their table. My presence at their table would have dropped the group's mean IQ by at least thirty points.

Of course, it was my insecurity with my appearance that made me feel unwelcome, but one of the nerdy girls said, "Don't make eye contact and don't even look at her. She ruined my experiment last month by contaminating the soil sample with soda."

I couldn't deny the accusation. With Chloe and the rest of my popular friends, there was no telling what we said and did throughout our reign. I vaguely remembered dumping my pop into a flower pot during science class, while my once-upon-a-time friends cheered me on. I probably did it.

Although I knew I deserved all of their rudeness, I fought the urge to yell at the nerds, "Go play with your nasal spray and leave me alone. I want to sit next to you and your calculators about as much as the crap-kicking cowboys. Look at you stuffing tofu and yogurt wraps in your brace-faces. I hope you all choke on it!!"

Then, I'd continue my tirade by turning to the cowboys' table and screaming, "Hey, all ya cowboy wannabes, ya'll can bite me! I don't care what ya'll think with your tight blue jeans and turd boots. I'd rather have this here hair than smell like cow turds..."

My verbal rampage ended in my head with me throwing up a middle finger to the whole student body. Flipping people off wasn't really something I was accustomed to doing. In fact, I'd never flipped anyone off in my life, but it would've been the perfect way to finish my angry tirade. It would've felt so good to stare down all of these idiots while flashing them the bird. Just as quickly as the urge came, in the same breath, it was gone. I'd never stoop to their level.

Moving toward my usual lunch table with my boyfriend, Keagan, and best friend Chloe, I waited to find out if they'd jump up and hug me. No one reacted. The cafeteria caved in on me. I continued to walk aimlessly, beginning to feel like hyperventilating. What would my obituary read?

Jett Wulff, 13, died suddenly from suffocation after being ignored at lunch. Her friends reported Jett came to school with a horrible haircut, and no one would talk to her.

Oh, wait. I didn't have any friends. They wouldn't report my death. Those who I thought were my friends would probably kick me in the stomach when I fell to the ground.

> The cafeteria ladies at Jefferson Junior High reported Jett Wulff, a homely, eighth grade student, tried to sit down at a table with a group of popular kids to eat the school's delicious stroganoff when she suddenly passed out. The only unusual signs left on the dead girl were a few stringy, black hairs remaining on her head. Police do not suspect foul play, since the cafeteria ladies did not witness anyone touch Jett or even speak to her for that matter. The cafeteria workers stressed again how wonderful their food was and the meal played no part in the girl's demise.

The local TV reporter was totally into the story. She was all about flipping her hair and getting high off of children's tragic deaths. The reporter smelled big ratings and a promotion to the evening news. I saw her standing right in the middle of the cafeteria, batting her eyelashes while she spoke dramatically into the camera:

"I'm here at Jefferson Junior High where police are investigating a suspicious death of an eighth grade student who fell over dead right here in the middle of the cafeteria. Police have tested the cafeteria food and have no reason to believe she was poisoned. Let's speak to some key witnesses here at Jefferson Junior High."

Before batting her eyelashes dramatically, the reporter would turn to my used-to-be best friend:

"Young lady, did you see what occurred here today?"

"Oh, yeah, it was like so mortifying! Jett used to be cool and was so fun to hang out with, but then she cut all of her hair off and dyed it and was like not cool anymore. We couldn't bear to look at her. She knew that was a bad idea."

Chloe started to cry, and the reporter put an arm around her to console her, but careful not to mess up her hair, as she pretended to care. She continued,

"Yes, we've heard, but did you see how she died?"

"No, we didn't even notice when she killed over, because once she wasn't cool, it didn't matter to us. We were all still in complete and utter shock about how BAD she looked. I mean her hair was HIDEOUS! Who would come to school with that HAIR?!"

Chloe continued to sob uncontrollably. The reporter moved on to interview Emily, who was in my science class. Emily adjusted her lopsided ponytail, poked her glasses back up the bridge of her nose, and responded matter-of-factly.

> "And what did you see?"
>
> "My highly intelligent friends and I were sitting at lunch, discussing the current healthcare movement and its impact on school lunches when this girl walked by us. She appeared to be walking in a blank gaze. We speculated if she were intoxicated or had ingested narcotics."
>
> "Drugs? Was this student known to be taking any drugs?"
>
> "No, we only speculated this possibility, but one of my friends identified the girl as one of the uncoolest girls in school. While we all admitted we felt sorry for her, we also expressed our excitement in having someone else to throw out to the wolves."

In my daydream, after speaking to Emily, the reporter decided apparently no one noticed or cared I laid dead in the middle of the cafeteria, so she moved on to a more important story like the traffic report.

Those at the top of the social ladder at Jefferson Junior High were like wolves. I knew, because I'd been one of them. The popular kids found prey around every corner, found their weaknesses, and continued to hunt them. My optimism faded when I arrived at the Ponies' table. We gave our group the nickname after reading *The Outsiders* in English class. We found the name very clever, since Ponyboy was so cute in the movie and since we all had long, beautiful hair we pulled up into ponytails.

All of the Ponies dramatically spread their lunches, which at times only consisted of a small bag of carrots and a diet soda, and waited to ignore anyone who didn't fit in our mold. So, when no one even looked up at me, as I turned away from our table to find a more secluded spot, I knew the outcast table was my next option. No judge and jury needed.

Chloe glanced up, as I turned away, and said, "Sorry, Lyla, no room at the inn."

She obviously tried to be funny, and, although there was no humor in it, her friends laughed hysterically. They all knew they were wrong, just as I had often laughed or cracked jokes at another's expense, knowing it was wrong. It didn't matter. The stakes were too high. I was a master at this game. Everybody does whatever you want them to do, or you make them feel stupid. If that doesn't force them to follow you, you do the unthinkable, you reject them and ignore them.

As soon as I looked in the mirror the first morning back to school with this hair, I should have known it was all over. Call me naive. As I approached my friends, I felt like the same Jett. Running my fingers through my new short crew cut, I responded, "Oh, okay. I get it. It's my hair."

"Ya think?" Chloe answered. "Do you really think we want to be around you when you look like a friggin' loser?"

Another girl chimed in, "Jett, you do look pretty disgusting. You look totally emo or deranged."

Keagan sat next to the girls silently. Any minute, I expected him to say, "Hey, guys, this is my girl! She looks beautiful with or without hair."

I just knew he would declare his love, stand up, and give me a long, passionate kiss. My expectations were smashed. Instead of helping me, he was too busy kissing his ham sandwich. The way he stared engrossed in his sandwich, it was apparent he didn't plan to say anything on my behalf. However, he batted his long eyelashes a piece of ham instead.

"Wow," I muttered. "I see how this is going to go."

My eyes burned a hole through the back of his head, and the jerk still ignored me. It was a tough act. After being a reject for years, I quickly recoiled. Again, I was a nobody. Their facial expressions, insincere laughs, and glances back and forth from me to one another told me my short claim to fame was over. They could make fun of my haircut all day long, but one thing I knew for sure was—I wasn't stupid. They hated me because of how I looked now.

"Well, screw you, Keagan," I spat at the cowlick on the back of his head, but he never turned around.

Another round of laughter followed me, as I left the table. Keagan was my boyfriend for the last three months, and he didn't say a word to defend me. He was such a coward. He was supposed to be the one person who loved me for me, the real *me*. He lied when he'd said I was beautiful no matter what I was wearing. If that were the truth, he should have still loved me, despite my black and pink, spiky hair.

When we were still dating, I drew his name with fancy letters and hearts all over my folder and his face covered my locker. I made a note to myself to rip them all out of my locker and burn them as soon as I could. I didn't ever want to see his cowardly face again.

My first true love, or so I'd thought. For the last three months, I photographed him, capturing his face from every angle. His name revolved in my mind at least a hundred times every day. My heart fluttered, when I found him waiting for me at my locker between every class. After all of this, he didn't even ask me what happened to my hair. Suddenly, just like that, I was invisible.

A kid from another table yelled, "Dead girl walking," as I moved away from my old table towards death row—the crooked table in the very back corner of the cafeteria. No one wanted to sit there, unless they had nowhere else to go. It was too close to the pungent cooks' lair and sat right next to the teachers' table. Often the table sat empty or with only one or two losers, eating at the table quietly, lost in their own loser worlds. Only Jefferson Junior High's outcasts ate lunch there, and I was headed its way. Each passing comment launched at me hit me right between the eyes like David's slingshot. The skeezers especially enjoyed flinging the stones.

Their remarks hit me harder than any others.

"Hey, Jett, did you have a fun weekend?"

"Looking good, mama."

"What's wrong, Jett? Can't find a place to sit?"

The insults snipped at me like shears cutting off my long, beautiful hair again and again. A little of me and long strands of hair fell to the floor each time somebody threw their rude comments. When I looked down at the ground, the hair wasn't hair, it morphed into more and more shards of sharp glass.

Neova went right along with them, snipping away at my soul. My dreams of being "someone" for once in my life plummeted to the bottom of an abyss after four months of living a fantasy. Dropping my tray onto the table, I sat motionless until the bell rang. I pulled my stocking cap back onto my head and hurried down the hallway to my fourth hour class, and moved throughout the rest of the day in a fog. Loneliness enveloped me, but it was better company than crowds of classmates who continued teasing me. I'd been a loner before, but it never felt like this.

Jett was trailer trash, daughter of a waitress, and who was now the ugliest girl in school. Just as quickly as my popularity floated to the top of Jefferson Junior High's social pool, it sank to the bottom. It was all over...my reputation, my popularity, my image, my coolness, and my relationship with Keagan. I had created this facade. I invented it, cultivated it, and harvested the fruits of my hard work. With one huge mistake, it was all over just like that. It was hard enough losing my best friend, Chloe, but I'd also lost my first boyfriend, Keagan.

Every time I saw him throughout the day and the following days, my heart felt like it was hit by a dump truck. Keagan didn't call me to tell me it was over. He didn't have to. He dumped me just by his lack of acknowledgement. Day after day, I repeated the routine, pretended to be invisible and sat through class.

When I got online, though, there was always evidence people knew I was still alive. Flick'r was full of nasty comments, spewing insults all over my page, my used-to-be friends' pages, and even the losers' pages.

You should just kill yourself and get it over with.
Don't pull a Jett and do something stupid!
You look about as dumb as Jett.

Jett–what in the heck happened to your hair? Did somebody run over your head with a lawnmower?! LMAO

Every time I read the comments, the weight piled upon me, heavier than the snow outside. The weight followed me everywhere in school every day. I was a cancer to the student body.

EMILY

Holy moly. Dr. Z's final diagnosis stumped me, which rarely happened. I never saw that one coming. Although the symptoms were indicative of a patient suffering from a heart defect, the woman actually succumbed to an allergic reaction. Her new hair shampoo contained peanut butter extracts, detrimental because of her peanut allergy. I definitely knew I needed to read up on anaphylaxis. *Dr. Z: Autopsy Uncovered* was my favorite television show, and I anxiously waited all day until 7:30 p.m. to watch the newest case.

My mother knew to have dinner made, served, and cleaned up by 6:30 p.m. This left one hour to finish homework and to review my Dr. Z binder before the show began. Luckily, the station provided previews for the upcoming show throughout the week, so I had a general idea of what the autopsy entailed. I spent the days leading up to the new series, researching as much as I could on the given topic prior to Friday night's episode. I kept detailed notes and articles organized alphabetically in my Dr. Z binder.

I spoke to Dr. Z throughout the show, as if I were his apprentice and allowed myself to use any notes during the show. However, using the internet was not permitted during the show. First, it would be unethical, and also it would mean I had to take my eyes off of the show, which could lead to missing evidence. I also logged the findings and my determination in my binder. Of the two-hundred and seventeen episodes I'd seen, I correctly determined the cause of death in one-hundred and ninety-three cases, which was a 0.8894 rate of solvability.

Dr. Z: Autopsy Reports actually didn't begin until 7:33 p.m. because of unnecessary commercials. Apparently, marketing executives believed the same audience attracted to watching Dr. Z cut into dead bodies also cared about waterproof mascara and the softest toilet paper on the market. I strongly believed those marketers "missed the mark."

Fixated on the flat screen television in our living room, I waited for the show to begin. Dr. Z's autopsies were all cases based upon real autopsy reports. Dr. Z was brilliant and perpetually dissected corpses to determine victims' causes of death. The challenge of solving the case was as fun as decrypting a crossword puzzle.

When I was younger, solving cases challenged my racing brain. Hours pursuing words and numbers in Sudoku or crossword puzzles, were my passion. Now that my intellect has expanded, to me the human body was nothing more than a fascinating puzzle. No matter what the cause of death, there's a constant variable in human autopsy cases. So, this was the biggest part of my life. All weekend, I re-watched Dr. Z to search for clues I missed with my laptop beside me to research any diseases or medical terminology. Last Friday's episode was the case of the sleeping girl.

This was what I did all day at school. Mentally, I reviewed autopsy cases and planned for the next show. While our teachers lectured or gave us assignments, I pretended to listen, but my brain recalled an article and counted down the days remaining before I'd be old enough to get an internship with our county coroner.

In fifth grade, with the help of my homeroom teacher, I wrote a letter to Mr. Cole, our county coroner, requesting to work with him throughout the summer to gain experience. I nearly bit off all of my fingernails waiting for his response. The sadness permeated my spirit when I read his response:

Dear Emily:

Thank you so much for your interest in serving your community in the capacity as coroner assistant. Unfortunately, this position does not exist at this time. I would love to have you come along to job shadow sometime, if you are interested.

However, for many different reasons, including the graphic nature of my job and patient confidentiality, your parents would have to sign a permission letter and you would need to be 16 years of age before you could ride along with me.

Until then, continue studying and growing your knowledge of the human anatomy, and get back in touch with me when you are of age.

Good luck in all of your endeavors!
Earnest Cole
Jefferson County Coroner

It would be another four years before I'd be sixteen and have the opportunity to job shadow Mr. Cole. The anticipation of this event, which certainly would be the highlight of my childhood, was too much for me to bare. Until then, I planned to do as Mr. Cole advised and study every piece of literature related to thanatology. When I finally worked with Mr. Cole, he would be amazed with my knowledge and hire me full-time. Approximately two weeks prior to my sixteenth birthday, I planned to mail the letter sitting in the top drawer of my desk. I'd already composed the letter, explaining to Mr. Cole I was sixteen years of age and prepared to serve as his voluntary assistant. It was already in an envelope, along with a letter my father wrote and signed for me, granting permission for me to work with Mr. Cole.

In the meantime, every day I raced through my school lessons as quickly as possible, so as to allocate the remaining time to my study of thanatology. Since the lessons at school were so easy and often repeated everything we'd learned the previous year, it was easy to speed through the work. Unfortunately, I'd read all of the nonfiction pieces in our school library relevant to this topic, as well as our town's public library. However, my father allowed me to take my tablet to school, so I daily downloaded different books on thanatology or any related topic.

My free time also consisted of conducting experiments on dead animals, when I was lucky enough to find road-kill or other unfortunate cadavers along the street or in the woods. The first time my mother caught me with a dead bird, she told me she was concerned with my unusual behavior. After I explained I was trying to diagnose the bird's cause of death using its postmortem state, she was fine with it. She wasn't thrilled about it, but my mom was quirky herself.

Finding dead birds in our yard, I realized, wasn't consistently fruitful. In order to increase my cadaver supply, I contacted the conservation department to request dead animals, but they denied my request. They said I was too young to determine whether or not the animal had a disease. I then asked my dad permission to buy a classified ad in the newspaper to help me find cadavers to use in my research. Dad said people would find this morbid. Shocked at his accusation, I explained learning from corpses one day would help me to diagnose living things. Finally, he agreed to take me once a week hunting for road kill.

Just in case I encountered any potential subjects throughout my daily life, I kept a small suitcase as my backpack and took it everywhere I went through school, hauling my textbooks and scientific materials. The roll-along backpack also included any necessary tools I would need, if I found something. I used my Levenhuk DTX 50 digital microscope, a birthday gift last month, to examine our collections. I was pretty sure I was the only seventh grade student at Jefferson Junior High who carried Ziploc bags, tweezers, a pocketknife hidden in a pencil case, latex gloves, a bottle of Hydrogen Peroxide, and a small bottle of hand sanitizer (in case I have to handle dead animals without medical gloves).

My happiest times were riding along with my dad up and down country roads, looking for dead animals on the side of the road. I stopped telling anyone at school, even my friends at lunch, because they said it was disgusting or weird. People didn't make sense to me. How were my scientific endeavors any stranger than painting your toe nails or putting bat feces on your eyelashes as mascara?

Several weeks ago at lunch, a new means of obtaining materials for my experiments crossed my mind. A girl who rode my bus named Jett walked by me at lunch. She also was in my science class. When she walked by my table with a brand new short haircut, I had an intriguing idea. I'd seen a documentary on the *Discovery* channel about the various uses of human hair for extracting DNA and other useful information.

In other research, I learned that one student from Nepal used human hair in his experiments, hoping to solve his country's energy shortage.

He created a method to use human hair in solar panels to conduct the electricity, instead of using silicon, which was far more expensive. The potential for using human hair in research was endless.

Before Jett had long hair, but now it was very short. Noticing this change in appearance, I contemplated the ways I'd be able to use all of her hair remnants. It took me a few days to get up the nerve to ask her. One day after she walked by, I tried to catch up with her to see if she had possibly kept her hair.

When I finally caught up with her, I stuttered excitedly, "Excuse me, Jett."

She turned to me hopeful, as if no one else had spoken to her all day.

"I was wondering," I continued, before I lost the chance again, "if I could possibly have the remaining hair from after you got your hair cut?"

Jett's reaction was not as I expected. Her face turned from hopeful to disbelief, "Are you serious?"

"Um, yes, I am," I responded. "Do you still have your hair? Or did you already donate it to a worthy cause, because you did have thick, beautiful hair?"

Jett's eyes welled up, and she stormed off down the hallway, saying, "You're sick. Leave me alone!"

NEOVA

Weirdo. Loser. Emo. Crazytrain. I was called every derogatory name possible throughout my two years in junior high. At times, the names bothered me, although I snickered at their comments or acted like I didn't even hear them. During other times, I shot evil looks back at the name-callers, so they knew I heard the slanderous names. I made paper voodoo dolls in the bullies' images and stabbed needles into their bodies each time they called me names. On other days, I walked down the hallway or across the cafeteria without hearing a word they said. I grew immune to their insults and dirty looks. Well, kind of immune. All of those other kids were so fake that I tried to tell myself they weren't worth the tears.

All of those other kids played their parts in the daily soap opera of Jefferson Junior High. It was hard to believe I once was friends with some of them. Chloe was my first friend in elementary school eight years ago. Our first day of kindergarten, I comforted her, as she had a crying fit when her mom left her at school for the first time. Even then, she bright green eyes and the best clothes, but her eyes leaked endless tears, and her thick, auburn hair pulled into pigtails. When I hugged and reassured her, she stopped crying. We spent every recess for several weeks, walking around the swings holding hands. My mom didn't seem too concerned when she dropped me off for my first day of school, and, honestly, I was glad to escape our dirty, small apartment in the hopes of getting two meals in one day. But I felt sorry for Chloe, because she seemed to really miss her mom.

Despite my contributions to Chloe and others over the years, now that we were in junior high, they all had amnesia. All they saw now was my chunky frame and unusual attire. When I got on the Internet at home, one luxury my mother couldn't live without, I expected to have several postings telling me how stupid or lame I was. It was as if the other idiots at my school had immediate access to a dictionary of insults. They sure were brave when they were online and typed feverishly assaults at me and my friends on a daily basis on any social medium they could find. The same kids, who I shared classrooms with since kindergarten, turned on me. As soon as we were old enough to realize who had money and who didn't, which didn't take long, I was on the outskirts of popularity. I still didn't know how Jett made her trailer-trash way into the "money" group.

The popularity mongers also misunderstood our clingy, overly affectionate relationships. I loved Mikayla and Say, but not in that way. We linked arms and marched to class as a united front against those pompous preps with perfect hair, accessories, and phones. The common denominator with the popular crowd was money…or the appearance of money. In social studies, we learned about feudal systems and the monarch's control of society during these historical periods. As far as I was concerned, times weren't much different. If you had money, you had power. Or at least that's how it was at Jefferson Junior High. All of this contributed to the reason I didn't understand how Jett was so quickly accepted by the fake, popular crowd who called themselves Ponies, which, by the way, I thought was a completely stupid name.

Linking arms with my two friends at school as we walked down the hallway reminded me of a game we played when we were little. The game was Red Rover. Two teams stood facing each other with linked arms and they took turns chanting, "Red rover, red rover, send Neova right over." Mikayla, Say, and me linked our arms tightly to protect us from the insults they threw at us. Their insults slammed, and, without our linked arms, I wouldn't have made it from class to class. With incoming name-calling and eye darts, if I didn't have my friends holding my arms, I knew I would sizzle and fade away into oblivion like a vampire scorched by the sunlight.

My best friend, Say, was much stronger than me. Her real name was Sarah, but she decided around the same time she started coloring her hair shades of *Pick-me-up Purple* and *Rockin' Red,* the name Say sounded much more interesting. Say could've made it a week without Mikayla and me by her side. Six different foster homes in three years trained Say to be a warrior. With a roll of her eyes, Say transformed from bubbly and happy to dark and dangerous. I knew I'd never be as strong as Say.

Say was like a pit bull puppy. She was friendly and cute, but she could turn at any moment. I kept her at arm's length just in case. In my black jeggings and "Free Nelson Mandela" T-shirt, I couldn't handle the constant barrage of slams like she could. They saw my fat roll, muffin top, hanging over my pants. I shouldn't have eaten a second donut this morning. I flipped my long, blue bangs in front of my eyes to hide the shame of my fat butt and pretended I didn't hear what they said about us.

Each step from our lockers to Mr. Hall's math class grew more strenuous, so I clung tighter to Say's arm. I never understood why the whole school hated us. We never claimed to conform to what they believed, or wanted to look like them. We never gave the appearance we cared what they had to say about us. Girls with fake laughs and tight, black yoga pants, muffled insults with their perfectly manicured hands, glared as we walk by every day.

Some of the cool girls didn't even try to hide their disdain for us. It was as if they took it personally we didn't choose to mold ourselves into their cookie cutter perfection. The mean girls blurted their insults loud enough for everyone to hear without considering our feelings between giggles. Others, who were braver or just wanted to get a laugh from their friends, bumped into us and dramatically exclaimed, "Yuck, I got cooties!"

It was just mean, and I didn't get them. I wanted to turn around and yell, "Leave us alone! We aren't bothering you!"

But I knew that our existence was what bothered them. They didn't like *different*. They liked everyone to look and to act the same. *They were boring*, I repeated to myself like a spiritual chant to keep from crying, as Mikayla, Say, and I played Red Rover between every class period.

BILLY

I ran all the way to the spot the bus picked us up and pulled on my coat. The zipper broke already, and I just got the dumb thing for Christmas. The church came to our trailer with a box of presents before Christmas break, but that mean 'ole Cheryl made us wait until Christmas mornin' to open 'em. Dumb Cheryl said Santa came early, but we still hadta wait. Me and Spare tried to ask Dad to let us open 'em, but he just pointed at dumb Cheryl and burped. Every night I dreamed of rippin' open the sparkly paper and findin' piles of toys and video games, more than I could even think of. There hadta be twenty presents each for me, Spare, and Nicki's baby, Bro.

Spare's my bigger sister in fourth grade, and when I said she's big, I meant it. She looked like a football player, and Sheryl called her spare tire 'cause of her fat belly. Sparrow's the real name our mama gave her. Spare called 'ole Cheryl cuss words behind her back when Cheryl called her spare tire. Nicki's my big sister who quitted school last year when her boyfriend left her. Her boyfriend done up and left 'er with 'nothin but a big belly. Cheryl said the last thing she needed was 'nother baby to take care of.

His name was Johnny, and Cheryl let him stay in one of the rooms with Nicki when they was a'goin together. He was purty nice to me, but now he's gone. Nicki just calls him Sonofagun now. Like she'll tell Bro, even though he cain't even walk, "Baby Bro, your daddy's a Sonofagun, and good fer you, you look like your Uncle Billy."

Hearin' uncle in front of my name makes me purty proud. Nicki's not even my real sister, 'cause Cheryl's her real mama, but she still lets me be an uncle. Cheryl's been runnin' our house since she moved back in when I went off to first grade.

Cheryl said, "I's the boss in this castle. If you don't like it, you can just get on over it."

So, Cheryl's been here for the last two years runnin' the show. I tried to ask my Dad where our mama went. Daddy tole me my mama went off to beauty school, but I heard Cheryl say dad was liein' at me. One day when Daddy was gone, Cheryl got mad at me for gettin' my pants dirty playin' outside.

Like she always did, she hollered at me, but this time, she was real meaner than ever. Cheryl yelled at me, "You ain't nothin' but a pain in my neck like yar no-good mama. No wonder yar mama left 'cause you's a pain."

I yelled back at Cheryl, "My mama left to go to school, and when she comes back, she's gonna be mad you stole her house and she's gonna kick ya on outta her. And my mama's way purtier than you too. Just ask my daddy."

Cheryl's face turned red, and she came swattin' at me like a wild boar, slappin' all the way and yellin', "Yar mama ain't at no school, you little dummy. Yar mama ran off with another man to work at a bar. And she ain't gonna send no money and ain't be coming back, boy, so get that there outta yar dumb, ugly head. I's the boss of this castle."

The mean things she said about my mama hurted worse than when she slapped at me, twisted my arm, or tooked the belt to my backside. I tried my best to always do good so she won't say bad things about my mama. I saved up all of my wild energy for the bus stop or for the playground at school. Most of the kids on the bus cussed and hit and talked about hatin' school.

I cussed right back at 'em and acted like I didn't wanna go to school neither. Deep down, I knew that's all a load of horsecrap. Mr. Mike pulled up with the bus, and I threw my handful of gravel at the little stray dog playin' with us and got on up on the bus. Yep, school's much better than home 'cause at school there ain't no Cheryl.

MRS. POWELL

Thirty-two years was a long time to be in the business. Every year, I told myself this was my last, but then I found my contract in my mailbox in the Spring. I signed it again every year, agreeing with myself and my husband the next year would be my last. I figured retirement would be easier than this. I'd seen my friends bow out gracefully year after year with a look of jubilation on their faces and with questions as to why I didn't also throw in the towel. With my kids grown and out of the house, I just didn't know what I'd do if I retired. When I was younger, I figured I would spend my retirement traveling to Paris and writing the next great American classic novel.

Now, my vision of retirement was attending the weekly *Quilting with the King* meeting. The Q&K ladies spent every Wednesday making a quilt for one of the church fundraisers in between reading scriptures and praying. Once in a while, the Q&K Club really spiced things up by listening to their favorite music from their youth. Thus, began the Q&K Club, a club dedicated to paying homage to its members' two heroes—Jesus and Elvis. All club members swore they only listened to Elvis' music prior to his drug abuse, so it didn't interfere with their heavenly walk. I tried to find excitement in these Q&K meetings the past two summers.

In between discussing the most recent scandals in town, Gladys Miller asked the group about the best home remedy for her hemorrhoids. This led to every woman in the group comparing their bowel movements, sores, infections, and any other problematic health issue they battled in secret. The thought of repeating this sacred, quilting ritual every week for the rest of my life brought the taste of bile to my mouth. Still seated at my teacher's desk, I glanced up at the magnetic mirror on my filing cabinet. Often, the mirror saved me the embarrassment of speaking to eighth graders with spinach in between my teeth or my slip caught in my pantyhose. A wrinkled face surrounded with white hair stared back at me from the mirror. *Who was that?* Every time I saw my reflection these days, it took a moment of recollection to realize—that old lady who looked just like my grandmother—was me. When did I get so *old?*

My free time, which was once spent with my daughter playing at the park or shopping for high heels with friends, would now be spent with other old women, sewing on an ornate, tacky quilt nobody wanted. On exciting days, I would reassure Bertha the podiatrist could scrape the corns off of her feet and taking my husband for his annual colonoscopy.

To top off the other downfalls of retirement and the possibility of joining the Q&K Club, the truth was I couldn't even sew. I had tried several times, and I couldn't even get thread through the needle and never had the patience to stitch more than three inches when someone else got the needle ready for me. I wondered why I had to follow the paths of every other retired woman in Jefferson County by sewing quilts and scheduling unending doctor appointments. Instead, I decided I might as well keep teaching, at least until I found a hobby I enjoyed. In the meantime, I had summers off, and I liked grading papers. Finding sentence fragments and marking up students' papers with my red pen gave me a strange thrill that no one would understand, if I tried to explain it to them. It was as satisfying as finishing the Sunday morning crossword puzzle.

And then there was my inexplicable connection with my kids. Each year a new group of naïve, young minds entered my classroom eager to learn how to successfully pen a Shakespearean sonnet. I prayed I meant as much to my students as they meant to me. Over the last thirty years, I learned more from the children than I ever dreamed of teaching them. It was to see their enthusiastic faces that I came to school each morning.

The eight o'clock morning bell reminded me today was a new day. Looking down at the scattered stack of three-ring binders, I knew I needed to get through at least a couple more journals before my students filed in for homeroom. Journal after journal, the students poured out their thoughts and frustrations in responses to my prompts. Some journals were usually fairly boring.

Last week, I posed the question, "What is the first thing you would do if you won the lottery?" Most students wrote they would go on an expansive shopping spree, buying the latest and greatest cell phones and cars. I should have known these children would write about cellular phones. If they weren't forced to put them away in class, their little noses were right in them like rats on stink. Some of my students' responses always were somewhat predictable. No matter what the question was one of my students, Emily, related it to the human anatomy and her fascination with carnage.

For example, one day, I asked, "If you were an animal, which animal would you be and why?"

While most students responded with the cliché answers of cats, dogs, koala bears, etc., Emily chose to be, of all things, a maggot. If Emily didn't regularly respond with unusual, outlandish answers, I may have been troubled. In her journal, she explained she would choose a maggot, so she would play an active role in decomposition of the human body after death. Emily added the significance of maggots in the decay process of animal carcasses and went into explicit detail on the decaying process. Emily's answers actually intrigued me, since her perspective on different topics was so very unlike any other student, or even my own, of such topics. One just never knew what Emily would write, or even say, for that matter.

Thus, when I questioned the class about how they would spend the money, if they won the lottery, I anticipated creative answers from both Emily and Jett. First, Emily answered she would use her winnings to purchase a fully supplied surgery center, which included enough cadavers to perform experimental surgeries. She added that she would open all cold cases in Jefferson County, employing numerous detectives and coroners to participate in investigations to attempt to solve the cases. Emily also mentioned something about lowering the age of students who wanted to hold coroner intern positions for the county.

If this written assignment was handed in by any other student, I normally would have been alarmed; however, my experience in education had taught me that it was normal for students with high-functioning autism to think differently than their classmates. They often focused on their individual interests and specific obsessions. Only a couple students wrote they would use the money to invest, to save, or to donate to their favorite charities.

One journal I was always anxious to read was Jett's. In response to every writing prompt, she wrote in great detail. To this particular prompt, Jett wrote:

If I won the lottery, I think it would be unbelievable. I haven't had much good luck in my short life. If I did win by chance, first, I would buy a house for my mom, and little brother, and me, and it wouldn't be a trailer. It would be a bright white house with a fenced in yard. The house would have three bedrooms and two bathrooms, and we would never run out of money for electricity. Since we didn't rent the house, for the first time, my little brother could finally have a puppy, and we'd name her Destiny.

Because of this incredibly lucky lottery ticket, my mom could finally quit working all of the times, or at least one of her jobs. Merl would probably quit the one at the restaurant, so she wouldn't come home sweaty every night and smelling like bacon and horseradish. We would use our winnings not only to buy a house, but we would buy a BRAND NEW car that never broke down, and we never would have to climb out of one of the windows to get out when the door jammed. Merl would drive us to and from school, so we wouldn't have to stand at a bus stop with a swarm of kids every morning.

If we had money for once, I'd never have to pretend not to be poor and, since I was rich, I'd automatically have tons of friends. Even if my hair was all messed up, I'd still be popular. For once, I wouldn't care either. Finally, if I won the lottery, I would hire a private detective to find my dad. I don't know exactly what I would do once I found him, but at least I would know who he was for real and what was so interesting that kept away from me. Since I had money, I could pay him to visit me…and maybe he and Merl would even fall in love again. Who knows? With that much money, the possibilities were endless.

Jett was one of those students who I knew I'd remember forever. Years down the road, I'd think back upon her journal writings and wonder where she was and what she had chosen to do with her life. As I read her response, it reminded me why I became a teacher in the first place. Helping kids like Jett was why I became a teacher. Her authenticity pulled at my heartstrings. Deep down, I knew Jett, and others like her, would never win the lottery or get an easy break in life. Unfortunately, I feared she would aspire to become something much greater than her future held.

One day less than ten years from now, I predicted, I would go out for dinner with my husband to the local diner, and Jett would be our waitress, serving us cold country fried steak. Jett would share with us pictures of her babies and how she planned to take night classes soon, when she had enough time. We would leave a big tip, because we felt sorry for her, and, all of the way back home after dinner, I would tell my husband about the amount of potential Jett had before she became another statistic. She'd be lucky to even finish high school.

This week's journal writing was a free writing assignment: "*What are you thinking?*"

Most of the boys wrote about their favorite video games or riding four wheelers. Most of the girls wrote about girl drama or which boy they liked this week. Once in a while, I read a journal with a passionate outburst about terrible parents or unfair punishments. Jett's journal entry this time was not the usual three-page ramblings that held my interest. Jett had a gift for articulation, so my first impression of her brief passage was she must have become distracted during the quiet writing time. However, once I read the couplet on the page, I knew Jett's brevity was intentional.

> One pink pill, two white pills, three.....and a handful more
> Take a few blue pills, drink water, and wait to hit the floor.

After re-reading the lines twice, my heart sank. Her recent journal entries were shaded with sad undertones, but they were never as dark as this. This was by far the most concerning entry she had ever written. I couldn't ignore this startling confession. Jett couldn't become another statistic; she still had time to escape that destiny.

CHLOE

Our conversations every morning on the way to school were always the same. If Mom drove me, I was forced to answer a million stupid questions about my friends and listen to her blab all the way to the school. "How is your friend, Josie?" "What about that Jett girl? I really liked her." "Are you and Dalton still talking?" Mom fired questions at me, as if she could squeeze a week's worth of conversation in the only ten minutes I saw her in a day.

She didn't even really listen to me anyway, which was obvious since she kept asking me about Jett. I'd told her a bazillion times already that I wasn't hanging out with Jett anymore. What was especially annoying was my mother's attempt with brattle was to cover up her obvious disinterest in my life. She didn't care about who my friends were or what I learned at school. All my mother was really concerned with was winning her latest case and looking good for Brad.

She smoothed a double coat of red lipstick across her lips in the rearview mirror. The urge to insult her wrestled inside of me. I wanted nothing more to insult her by telling her red lipstick was so 1990's and she looked like a clown. Sometimes, I didn't fight it and allowed myself the pleasure of insulting my mother, making cracks about her low-cut shirts or hooker stilettos.

In return, she half-heartedly grunted her favorite saying, "Teenagers today are so rude."

If my dad drove me to school, the ride was much different. The entire fifteen-mile ride was silent, except the blabbing broadcaster on dad's *National Public Radio* station. If dad was in a particularly good mood, he talked some, but he spoke to the radio announcer enthusiastically, not me.

"Are you kidding me?" he asked the announcer. "I didn't know that. Da Vinci invented the first armed tank? I knew about the flying machine he drew, but not the tank or a submarine. The man was a genius."

Next to accounting and talk radio, my dad loved classical art, music, and literature. He spoke about these interests to himself, but sometimes I listened to him out of boredom. Every morning when he drove me to school, it was the same routine when dad pulled our Lexus in front of Jefferson Junior High. As I unloaded from the luxury vehicle, and other students gawked, my dad muttered his routine, "I'll be back after school to pick you up at 3:15 sharp. Don't dilly-dally. Don't make me wait. See 'ya then. Oh, and, um, love ya."

After slamming the door shut, adjusting my hair and outfit, and walking away from my father without another word, I mouthed to myself, "Yeah, love you too, dad," and set it all off with a conclusive eye roll.

The painful drives to school with dad often made me sympathetic to mom's interest in Brad. My dad was about as much fun as playing with a rabid raccoon. Did my father really not know about mom's boyfriend? Or did he really not care? I knew for a fact, he must've had some sneaking suspicion. Last week, he answered mom's cell phone when Brad called. From what I overheard, Brad fed Dad some crap about working with mom on an upcoming case. Brad lied and said he needed to ask her about lost dispositions.

When Dad hung up, he stood emotionless and stared into the burning wood fireplace. Without any comment, he walked over and jabbed the fiery logs forcefully several times, causing little embers to shoot back at him. Several other sparks cascaded onto an arca rug in front of the fireplace. Dad stomped them out. His forceful kicks was the most energy exerted from my dad, since he lost his favorite calculator three years ago. After wondering, if I felt sorry for him or disgusted by his weak response, I resolved I was indifferent. Both of my parents were so selfish, they didn't deserve any emotional response from me.

My dad's problem was he was the stereotypical accountant. Back when my mom appeared to still like my father, she'd tell me how they met in college in Statistics 101. Mom said Dad's ability to quickly figure the problems, as well as his green eyes, first impressed her. When mom got to know him better, she said it didn't hurt when he let her cheat off of his homework and that his parents were well-off. My mother also told me it took nearly six months before my dad asked her out.

From the first time my mother told me this story years ago to the last time I asked her, the story morphed from a pleasant memory to my mom's recent reflection.

She said, in her perfect prosecuting attorney voice, "I should've known I wasn't marrying the most exciting man on the planet. I chose boring and dependable. I just wish I was as intriguing as balancing a budget."

My mom turned away from me, took a deep breath, and moved toward her bedroom with a conclusive, "Oh, well, too late now. I'm going to take a warm bath."

Glancing over to my father, as he drove me to school with both hands on the steering wheel, I admitted he wasn't exactly the easiest person to talk to. Sure, my dad was successful and handsome, and he had great hair. But his biggest joys in life were keeping a detailed spreadsheet of household bills and watching *The Weather Channel.* Need I say more? Maybe my dad didn't know my mom found another man. Or maybe my dad was afraid, if he brought the subject up, he and mom would argue and his daily routine would be disrupted? We knew he couldn't stand an account that didn't balance.

I just about let myself start to care. I rolled my eyes, although my father obviously didn't even notice. Whatever. I had my own problems to worry about... like if Keagan would be waiting for me on the sidewalk when dad dropped me off at school. Sometimes I wished I rode the bus to school to avoid this boring drive altogether.

Sometimes when both of my parents had morning appointments, I was forced to ride the bus. I used to sit with Jett, and we caught up on the latest gossip and talk about our weekend plans. Since we weren't friends anymore, though, I don't know who I'd sit with. My dad surprised me by attempting again to start up a conversation.

"So, Chlo, what happened with your one friend who used to come over to the house all the time, the one with the long blond hair?" my dad asked. "She hasn't been over for a long time? The one named like an airplane. Did you girls have a squabble?"

"Really, Dad? *Squabble?*" I responded. Why all of a sudden was my dad so interested in my social life. "It's not like we are eight years old. No, we didn't have a *squabble.* We just grew apart. We don't have anything in common anymore."

"Well, she was such a nice girl and good manners," Dad said. "You two seemed to be really close."

"No, dad," I answered with annoyance. "We quit hanging out a long time ago."

I didn't want to get into details with him. He wouldn't have understood anyway. Dad seemed satisfied with my answer and finished our morning commute to school. Once I finally escaped the depressing commute to school, my dad's continuous yawning and watching the digital clock on the dash of our Lexus, I felt a weight lifted off of my shoulders. I slid out of the car very carefully, so as not to not wrinkle my purple suede skirt and moved ever so slowly gathering my backpack to annoy my dad. My dad was notoriously always in a hurry.

"Let's go, Chlo, you know I need to get to work," he said, as he did every morning. "Aren't you going to be cold in that skirt?"

Looking down at my outfit, it was obvious my dad just now really looked at me and what I wore. He was way too into Leonard daVincent, or whoever he was, and hanging out with his radio announcer.

"Sorry to be such a pain and make you late for an important meeting," I responded in my most disrespectful tone. "Way to go, Dad, you noticed what I was wearing! I have tights on underneath. Bye!"

With a final slam of the car door, I moved towards the front of Jefferson Junior High. Everyone watched me with jealous eyes. They all wished they had the same outfit I wore. One perk of not seeing my parents much was that when they were around, they always gave me whatever I wanted. They thought a credit card and presents made up for my nightly dinners alone. Being the only child of a wealthy accountant and attorney, I had everything I wanted. For some reason, though, I often felt empty. I would've traded all of the gifts and freedom for parents who pretended to care a little.

Out of loneliness or anger at my parents, I took advantage of their guilt, getting everything I wanted and treating them like dirt. You'd think I was used to being home alone all of the time by now. I paced the hardwood floors looking at fancy, expensive furniture my parents worked all of the time to buy, but never sat in. It didn't make a whole lot of sense to me.

Many times I wanted to take a butcher knife and to slash the leather sofas my parents spent ridiculous amounts of money on. The chairs often sat empty, reminding me of how I felt in our "home." Sitting at the granite counter top eating microwave dinners made me feel empty.

Watching prime time television in an empty, but gorgeous living room, made me feel empty. Even when my dad was home, he stayed in his office on his computer, which made me feel even emptier.

Now I had Keegan though. I had something to look forward to. Just like every day for the past two weeks of school, Keagan waited for me next to the bench in front of the school. Jett and I used to meet at the same bench next to the front door. An ounce of guilt almost bubbled in my stomach every time I saw Keagan, because he was Jett's boyfriend before. Once Keagan stared down at me with his piercing green eyes, I forgot feeling sorry for her. Oh well, the way I saw it, it was her own fault she lost Keagan to me. She never should have gone out with him to begin with. She knew I liked Keagan since the fifth grade. She wasn't even living here then. A real friend didn't go after her best friend's crush.

After the hair incident, Jett should've known a boy like Keagan would dump her. No one expected Keagan to keep her as a charity case. She turned into a weirdo. He couldn't stay with a girl who looked like a deranged lunatic. It was one thing she changed her hair, but then she started to dress like a slob.

There were several theories in the rumor mill about her haircut. One rumor going around over Christmas break. Some people said she turned psycho, tried to stab her mom with scissors, and her mom cut her hair off as punishment. The other rumor was Jett got high and changed her hair to look more punk-rock, but her makeover didn't turn out as she planned.

When everyone asked me, I shrugged and responded, "It's not like we were best friends or something."

Jet missed school all of the time now. The bubbly, laughing girl I knew was gone. She even stopped wearing the name-brand hand-me-downs I gave her. Since my closet was packed full, I'd given her some of my clothes, when I noticed she wore some of the same clothes. No one really wore the same outfit twice in the same month. What I hadn't expected was my little protégé to become more popular than me.

Oh, well. Jett's loss was my gain, I thought, as I walked into school, holding Keagan's hand. Another day of school meant another day I spent back on top. I looked down to make sure no lint had collected on my skirt or tights, before I put on my popular *Chloe* face.

THURSDAY

JETT

Even the first day in this new school wasn't this bad. On the first day of school, the Ponies embraced me without question. When you had long hair, the options were endless—messy bun, glamorous curly down-do, pulled to the side with a sparkly head band, straightened into a flat perfect blanket of beauty, or pulled high and tight in a ponytail. The Ponies never knew the meaning of a bad hair day. For the first part of this year, I was one of them. My hair cooperated perfectly every day. The one thing my unknown biological father gave me was a thick, luscious mane of hair, so I fit right in.

At my last school, after one day, the popular kids learned where I lived, so I never had a chance at being cool. Here at Jefferson Junior High, though, everyone lived a ways from school. Everything was so spread out. Where you lived didn't matter as much. I learned what really mattered was looking good and being popular.

My long, thick, sandy blond hair and easy smile bought me a ticket right up to first class with the Ponies. My first day at Jefferson Junior High was a breeze. As soon as I walked into homeroom, the Ponies clung to me. Before third hour, I was one of them, laughing at their jokes and sitting with them at lunch, as if I'd always been one of them. For once in my life, I was on top. I was popular.

Years of moving from school to school taught me to adapt like a chameleon. In my previous schools, I blended in, but my goal when we moved again, two hours away from our last home town, was to make it into the popular crowd. I achieved greatness. By the second day at my new school, I knew the ropes already. The rules to popularity were the following:

1. **Don't act too smart, but not too dumb**. If the Ponies know you're smart, they will think you are showing off. You don't want to look dumb either. It's a difficult balancing act.
2. **Look good every day**. Not only do you need to look good every day, but every minute of the day. You never knew when someone might take a picture of you.
3. **Avoid the losers.** They were easy to find. They clung to their friends, wearing matching *Hello Kitty* barrettes and covered their dark eyeliner with long bangs.
4. **Less was more.** Act like you didn't care what anybody thought.
5. **Never let anyone see where I really lived**. Act like you live in a normal subdivision not a trailer park. Make fun of people of the kids who lived in junky houses.

Luckily, ours was one of the first bus stops every morning, so we were already on the bus when the bus picked them up. The other kids who got on the bus there never questioned where we lived. Sammy and I snuck around the back, maybe a quarter of a mile, and walked up to the bus stop, as if it were our own. No one asked. They must have assumed we came from another similar subdivision of nice houses. Many of my friends' parents drove them to school every day. Riding the bus, though, wasn't that bad. Our bus driver, Mr. Mike was so nice to all of us; I had a sneaking suspicion that he knew we got on at the wrong bus stop.

Every morning, he greeted me with the routine, "Mornin', Joan Jett."

Next to what you looked like, who your friends were, and where you lived, the next important staple in popularity was Internet access. Every day we all congregated on Flick'r, the coolest social media site at Jefferson Junior High. With one click, any junior high student could lose every ounce of social status at Jefferson. Everybody who was anybody had their column on Flick'r. We all uploaded the best pictures and posted our daily happenings in the "What's up?!" section. Another Flick'r feature popular with all of the Ponies, and wanna-be Ponies was the video game feature. The site allowed for you to type in names and descriptions, and by completing a brief questionnaire, you had a totally original, unique video game. Then all of your friends played your game and left comments.

My photography added another element of coolness to my popularity. My pictures of my friends looking their best and in unusual settings had everyone wanting to be my friend, so I'd take their pictures. I posted pictures of all kinds of things. They were good, and I knew it. My relationship status with one of the cutest guys in school, Keagan, didn't hurt my popularity either.

Along with everyone else who aspired to be popular, I spent much of my free time online, posting pictures to make me look better than everyone else or by browsing everyone else's pictures and comments. If you didn't quickly click "flickin' cool" next to your friends' deepest, dimwitted thoughts and decadent selfies, they questioned your true commitment to the friendship. We all knew the depths of our fakeness, but played along any way.

My new image was a transformation from my old self. I learned the hard way that in order to fit in, I needed to become a chameleon. Four schools ago in fifth grade, our teacher made us write a short essay on an animal. While my classmates chose different breeds of dogs, koala bears, and lions, I chose the chameleon. I learned it changed its color depending on its environment and emotions. Like the chameleon, I learned to adapt to my surroundings, which made my life easier and kept predators from approaching me, since I was nearly invisible.

I sketched chameleons when I was really bored and memorized the definition:

"The relative importance of the classes of chameleons function varies with the circumstances as well as the species. Color change signaled a chameleon's physiological condition and intentions to other chameleons. Chameleons tend to show darker colors when angered, or to scare or intimidate others."

At Jefferson Junior High, I became a chameleon—but a cool chameleon, looking like everyone else. However, after all of my progress in popularity, one bad decision erased it all with one snip.

After what those girls did to me, there was no way to blend in like a chameleon, no matter how hard I tried. Yesterday, Sammy got mad at me for not getting him up to go to school. Although my little brother didn't usually stay mad with me for too long, even a brief moment of knowing he was disappointed in me was too long. To Sammy, I was more than a mother than Merl, if you were to consider how much time I spent with him. When Sammy took a bath, learned his alphabet, remembered to brush his teeth, it was me who was there. As much as I tried not to, I still blamed Merl. She had to work to pay bills, but she could have tried harder. These were the thoughts I pushed to the back of my mind, as I took care of Sammy every morning and every night.

Without the responsibility of this precious little boy, I would have disintegrated. Sammy was the only reason I woke up to go to school half of the time—when I was kind of cool at our last home before Jefferson Junior High, when I was way popular at Jefferson Junior High, and, definitely, when I was not cool at all at Jefferson Junior High. The last thing I needed right now was to add Sammy to the list of people who hated me. So, I climbed out of bed, just for Sammy. Not only so he wouldn't be mad at me, but because it was the right thing to do. Sammy couldn't fall behind in school.

He was just learning to read and write. If it weren't for Sammy, I knew, I would have skipped every day before and after the hair incident. This because especially true after my hair was cut off. Years ago, I went to Sunday school with one of our neighbors who lived next door to us in a trailer park much like Todd's Trailer Garden, but in a different town. The sweet little girl's name was Sheila, and she invited me to go with her on the church van.

It's funny how I remembered her as a little girl with auburn hair and freckles, since she was the same age as me, but I remembered her as a little girl. In my memories, I was still the same, stagnant adolescent, but with hair. The Sunday school teacher told us a story about a very powerful man, using a felt board and Velcro characters. Mrs. Robbins was her name I remembered, and she spoke animatedly about the Bible characters.

The powerful man, she said, was named Samson, and he had long black curly hair. Samson was stronger than any man in his time. He killed whole armies by himself and was feared by everyone. The teacher also described Samson's heroic feat of killing a lion. Another Bible story, I'd heard somewhere, was about another guy who killed a lion, so half of Mrs. Robbin's lesson was spent contemplating in my young mind how there were so many lions running around. The ending was the only other part I remembered about Samson's story. His wife tricked him and cut off his hair while I slept, which took away his source of strength.

Later, his wife's family poked out his eyes and made him a slave, so his life was much worse than mine, but, at times, I felt like Samson. I dreaded seeing people, or them seeing me. Although I spent my time at home marinating in reality television, I concluded my new life was far more depressing than what those people had to endure. A roach for breakfast? I'd munch down on a roach or fly rather than go to school to face them. Living vicariously through the lives of rich housewives on TV, who stressed out over which lipstick to wear, appealed to me much more than going to school. These women dressed their pet pigs in frilly outfits worth more than our trailer, so I knew their lives would have been much better.

Nope. I didn't feel bad about skipping school. It was much easier to sleep in and to lay on the couch watching stupid TV rather than deal with the superficial pigs at school. You would've thought those morons, whom I used to call friends, would've grown bored of tormenting me and would've found a new victim. They hadn't. I ran my fingers through the short puff of hair, sitting on the top of my head.

One of the women on *Really Rich Wives* had like fifty wigs. They were all the same shade of blonde, but were in different styles, so all she had to do was put one on. You couldn't even tell it was a wig, which gave me the idea to buy a wig to cover my horrible haircut.

The reporter on another one of my favorite shows, *Famous and Fashionable,* interviewed the pop star, Lyla Stag. Lyla talked about the recent changes in her life and how she decided to makeover her appearance to reflect her life-changes. How was it Lyla shaved her head and stayed just as famous?

"Not every girl has been through the heartbreak and emotional rollercoaster Lyla has experienced," according to the melodramatic television host. "Lyla didn't let her situation get her down. When was ready to shed the pain and shame of a cheating fiancé, she took a visit to her hairstylist."

The camera cut to Lyla with her new boyish hair-cut, striking a pose on the red carpet in a bikini top and short shorts. Lyla told the reporter:

> "Yo, I not only was ready to break free from this bad relationship, but I wanted to ditch the stereotype that was buggin' me. My hair represents the new me. I'm growing up, peeps. It's tough for all of us, but I'm all good. No worries. I look hip, and I got a new boo."

A hunk who looked vaguely familiar stood by Lyla's side with his arm draped over her. He nodded and winked at the camera, which made me think he no longer was a hunk. The reporter screeched her last comments after a long hug with Lyla,

> "Most of you remember Lyla from the Disney television series *Lyla's Life*, but Lyla obviously is all grown up now. We wish you the best, Lyla."
>
> Like Lyla, I, too, recently endured a bad break-up, but it wasn't use that as my excuse for my horrid hair. I didn't think it looked good on Lyla either. No matter how famous she was, you had to have a certain shape of face to pull off this look.

To me, Lyla's finished product looked like my old, one-legged Barbie doll after Sammy played beauty shop with her. I didn't particularly mind Sam chopping off Barbie's hair. I was more concerned with his excessive interest in my dolls. As for Lyla's new 'do, I agreed with half of the world that it was hideous. But, of course, Lyla was a celebrity, so she got away with it.

Looking over into the gold speckled mirror, hanging in our trailer's living room, I thought, "Lyla, you should've known those girls would do this to you."

The reflection stared back at me with unfamiliar eyes, although I'd seen the same face for the past month. Short, bleached blond hair with pink and black streaks sat on my head. Now it was growing out a little bit, and the hair-do transformed into a shaggy Mohawk.

As for the color of my hair, it looked like I spilled black ink and Kool-Aid on my head. I looked cheap, and I knew today was going to be another rough day. Although it was a month since my haircut, it felt like eternity. Gone were the pictures of me with my friends that used to wallpaper in Sammy's bedroom. I took them down, so they wouldn't constantly remind me what I used to look like when I was pretty—back when I was popular.

The first four months at Jefferson Junior High were a dream. Three evil girls stole my dream, and I just counted down the days for school to be out. I relived what happened several times a day, but couldn't tell anyone. Merl thought I was going through a phase, so she didn't say a whole lot about my hair. Those girls deserved whatever they got in life, and I prayed it would be as bad as what I went through.

Hatred and revenge were venom through my veins. Regret joined the poison at times, reminding me I was the stupid girl who went over there that night. I should have known when I returned to school with this hair, my so-called friends would ignore me and treat me like a fungus. We treated everyone in our class who wasn't in our clique like they were dirt. Deep down, I knew they wouldn't accept me with my new mullet. It was only one semester of being their friend, but I witnessed a multitude of sins—name calling, teasing, judging—and I took part in it all.

My personal favorite was, "Hey, Lyla, did you have a little accident with the blender?"

As I walked their way towards my locker, they all looked at me and broke into laughter, which was familiar to me as the 'laughter' of making someone else feel stupid in front of others. Before my fall, I participated in the same cruel, condescending group laughter. It was the laughter we used, when we saw someone below us on the food chain who was vulnerable, and we were ready to pounce on her weakness.

"Is that a new 'do, or is that a skunk on your head, Jett?" Chloe screeched in between explosive giggles. I knew everyone else would follow Chloe's lead, slamming the final nail in my social coffin.

"She must think she looks like a rock star now," Mia whinnied like a horse.

"Yeah!" Sophia agreed. "Jett must wanna be just like Lyla Stag!"

Thus, there was the birth of my new nickname, Lyla. I stood before them humiliated. My life was never a carnival ride, but I was at rock bottom. Merl was working more than ever, my brother Sammy preferred playing with dolls and imaginary friends to me, and even our neighbors hated me.

Since it took thirteen years for my blonde hair to grow down to the middle of my back, I knew it would be a long time before it returned. After hearing the echoes of my classmates calling me Lyla Stag, I also knew it would be a while before anyone would call me Jett again.

People asked me all of the time how I got my name "Jett." I told most people my father was in the Air Force, and I never knew him. I told them that right before he died in combat saving the life of another soldier, my mother got pregnant with me. My name was a tribute to my late father, the jet pilot, who gave his life honorably during the war.

I told the story so many times I almost believed it myself. I saw my imaginary father in uniform, dodging bullets and carrying his comrade out of harm's way. In my make-believe story, my dad, who had big muscles and my same blue eyes with a hint of green, was injured in a helicopter crash. In my imagination, my father emerged from the wreckage when the enemy shot him straight through the heart.

As he fell gracefully to the ground, he uttered his final words to his co-pilot, "Tell my daughter I named her Jett, because I loved her even more than flying....and" (groan and gurgling sound) "tell my baby girl, daddy will always be with her."

Fabricating stories about my father, whom I no longer recalled, eased the pain of not knowing for sure who he was. Once in a shoebox in Merl's closet, I found a faded photograph of a man in a uniform. The smiling young man held a baby, who I assumed was me.

I gathered up the courage to ask Merl, and answered, after looking around the room, "Really, Jett? You just have to know everything, huh? It's all in the past. Yes. Yes, that was your father. Does that make you feel better knowing what he looked like?"

I stood dumbfounded. After all of these years, Merl admitted who my father was. She didn't give him a name, but I now had a face for my imaginary legends.

"Well, do you feel better?" Merl continued.

Merl spoke in her jaw-clenched voice, but I didn't care. My father was handsome and held *me*. He held *ME* smiling. And he looked like *me*.

"Yes," I answered. "I feel better."

As I stared at the picture, Merl ripped it from my hands and finished, "Well, I hope you're proud of him. He was too worried about himself to take care of us."

The words bit and stung my heart, and I never asked her about him again. When I thought of my father, though, I knew he held me once and looked happy. Of course, Merl told us a little about our fathers like that they both were losers, spent time in prison, and dead-beats. Her favorite name for them was "sperm donors."

The names once bothered me, but not anymore. Just as it once bothered me when I stared out the window, imagining my father would drive up out of nowhere. Sammy sometimes stared out the trailer window, and I knew he was watching for his father. I used to stare out the trailer window at passing cars, thinking that at any moment one of our fathers might pull up in a brown, bruised pick-up truck. We stopped watching out the window.

No one knew the truth about my name. Merl's reason for picking the name was far too embarrassing to explain. Merl's mom, my grandmother we rarely saw, spent most of the eighties as a groupie, chasing rock stars. One of her favorite musicians was Joan Jett. Merl said when she continued the family tradition and got pregnant at sixteen, my grandma talked her into the name.

Merl later admitted she never really liked the name, but thought it would be cool if she named me Jett and I came out with dark hair.

This was but another disappointment I caused for Merl. Unfortunately, I wasn't the dark-headed baby she hoped for. The little hair I was born with was as white as the delivery room walls. All of this twirled in my mind like the ballerina in the jewelry box grandma gave me for one of my birthdays. It was the only present she gave me, unless you counted my name.

The screaming alarm clock brought me back to the couch where I dozed in and out of slumber and bad memories. With my snooze button exhausted, I lifted myself off of the couch. Going back to school meant being treated like a leper.

As much as it hurt seeing my old best friends betray me, my grades were totally horrible after skipping school. I quietly treaded down the hallway to Sammy's room, careful not to wake up Merl, since she had pulled another all-nighter at her second job. Just as I was named after a rock-n-roll icon, my little brother was blessed with the same good fortune. He was named after Sammy Hagar, another one of grandma's favorites. After my mother told me the story about how she named my little brother, I had to Google Sammy Hagar to see who in the world he was and if he deserved to share a name with my angelic little brother.

When I went into Sammy's tiny bedroom to wake him up, he looked so small and innocent curled up on his stained, worn mattress. Just as I found him every morning, Sammy was on his belly in the middle of the mattress with his thumb in his mouth, hugging RaRa, his stuffed rabbit, a gift from the Easter bunny a couple years ago. He didn't have the car bed he wanted and his mattress nearly covered the entire room, but I let him have the second bedroom. I tried to make his life as normal as possible, while I slept on our used, lumpy couch in the living room.

It was the first time Sammy had his own bedroom for the first time in his life, so I didn't mind at all sleeping on the couch. We ended up sleeping together almost every night anyway. Sammy's bad dreams to seek me nearly every night, so when I tucked him in, he often asked me to sleep with him. It was more comfortable to cuddle up with his little soft body anyway. The few times I fell asleep on the couch, in the morning, I found Sammy beside me asleep on the living room floor with his hand up next to my hair.

Trying to awake him, I knelt next to his little, peaceful body and gently nudged his shoulder.

I whispered in his ear, "Hey, bubby, time to get ready for school."

Unzipping the sleeping bag, I lifted him into my arms, and his eyes slowly unfolded. My baby brother was growing heavier every day. I didn't want to think about the day when I couldn't lift him, but he would lift me.

Rubbing the sleep from his eyes, Sammy asked, "Are we gonna go to school today?"

"Yep!" I answered, faking excitement for his benefit. "We are going to learn all there is to learn."

"I'll get to see Ms. Collins!" Sammy said.

Sammy and I never even came close to receiving the *Perfect Attendance Award.* At the beginning of this year, I never missed a day of school. When you're on top of the world, you didn't want to miss a minute of the view, but now there was no desire to return. I was accustomed to the inquisition on the day we returned after missing a day or two of school. In my younger years, when we missed a lot of school, I felt guilty telling the teachers why I wasn't at school. I teared up, shrugged my shoulders, and stared at the floor until teacher grew bored with my silence.

When I got a little older, I found it was better to feed sympathetic teachers fake family dilemmas. Throughout the years, I reported recurring flat tires, three bouts with salmonella poisoning, influenza of every sort, and every other disease known to mankind, and nine dead grandpas. My personal favorite excuse for being absent was the time I told my teacher my Uncle Darrell (I never really had an Uncle Darrell) abducted me and tried to collect ransom from my long-lost millionaire father. The teacher's eyes grew big, as I described how he locked me in the basement with rats that nibbled on my toes.

Unfortunately, the twist to this story was my wealthy father never appeared to pay the ransom. So, my impatient, deranged Uncle Darrell sent me back to Merl to avoid prison time. During attendance, teachers nodded and moved on to the next student on the roll without much concern.

Missing school at Jefferson Junior High proved to be more difficult. One of my teachers, Mrs. Powell, was so nice and seemed to actually care when I didn't show up at school. I didn't admit to her that Sammy and I spent the day sleeping, watching TV, and reading. Most of my teachers wouldn't believe I loved to read. I made fairly decent grades, better, of course, when I chose to go to school, but I never got close enough to anyone for them to understand me. When Mrs. Powell looked at me, though, I could tell, she "got me."

Last week, after we missed a few days, Mrs. Powell peered down at me through thick, black rims and asked me if something was wrong at home or at school. I wanted so badly to tell her the truth and tell her everything. If she said anything about Chloe and the others, though, I knew it would only get worse.

"No," I lied. "Nothing's wrong. I've just been sick a lot. The doctors think I might have mono or something."

"Do you think your mother could come in to visit with me?" Mrs. Powell asked. She wasn't going to let it go that easily. "Your grades have dropped, and I want to share some concerns with her."

"Oh, um," I stammered, "I'll ask her, but I doubt she can make it. She's working a lot and she doesn't like to be bothered."

We both knew I suffered no physical ailments. Since I kept up on my missing work easily, there wasn't much the teachers could do, except threaten me. Mrs. Powell finally allowed me return to my desk, but I knew I couldn't miss much more school. Lying to my favorite teacher was too hard.

After finishing our twenty-minute morning ritual before school, we grabbed Pop Tarts and began our trek to the bus stop, at the end of the park to wait with the other trailer rats. Since losing my position with the Ponies, I gave up walking the three blocks to our fake bus stop. It no longer mattered where I lived. After my haircut, Chloe also found out where I really lived. She made sure everybody at school knew we lived in a run-down trailer with foil on the windows that kept in the heat.

Waiting for our bus, the Smith boys, who lived in trailer with sheets as windows, ran circles around a tree playing tag, while another group of kids threw gravel at a stray dog. Someone dumped the poor thing at the trailer park the week before.

The abandoned dog probably thought, "Thanks, master. Not only did you kick me out of our house, but you dumped me in the nastiest place in town. Now I get to spend the rest of my life eating out of trash dumpsters and getting tortured by booger-eating seven-year-olds?"

Yet, at the same time, the dog seemed to believe he played a game with the ornery boys. It probably hurt to be hit by small rocks, but the attention, even if it was negative attention, erased the sting of each pebble rocket. After watching the chaos of our bus stop for a few minutes, I felt a strange connection with the stray dog. Like him, I knew how easily we fell into a charade of having false friends who turned on you and cast stones. Little Billy, who lived two trailers down, stood staring down at the ground as usual with pocketed hands shoved into his filthy, too-small coat.

It was too cold for us to wait all of this time for the bus, but we didn't have much of a choice. As I exhaled thick, white puffs of air and shivered, I wrapped my arms around Sammy. He was getting so tall; his nose nearly reached my neck now. We both were instantly warmer. Waiting for the bus, I recalled the numerous trailers we called home over the last ten years. This was the eighth trailer we called home.

Every move meant a new town and a new beginning, but it also meant a similar trailer. Every one of them was adorned with a mirror installed to lend a façade of classy decor that contrasted the outdated, brown-paneled walls. Merl refused to call them trailer parks. She referred to each new home as a "modular home."

This pretentious title usually was followed by tirades about our dads and how their child support, if they bothered to pay a dime, we would have been able to afford to rent a real house. I wasn't holding my breath. I gave up on dreaming about living in a "real" home many years ago.

Our newest "modular home" was nestled quaintly in the middle of fifteen others and surrounded by a dilapidated chain-link fence. Driving by, the trailers looked like a fleet of docked ships, unloading gnarled pit bulls, overflowing trash bags, and smashed aluminum cans. According to Merl, short for Merlene, our trailer was advertised as the nicest in the park, so she signed the lease before taking a tour.

Merl added that her newest place of employment, Dolly's Diner, was only half-a-mile away, so the trailer was the perfect location for us, not to mention free trash pick-up and free Internet. What else did a modern family need?

"Think of the gas money we'll save," Merl said, carrying our plastic bags of clothes, last August when we moved.

I knew the truth. Merl ended up walking to work most of the time. Our car's gas tank lived on empty. That poor 1999 Honda Accord puffed fumes like a broke drug addict most of the time, threatening to leave us parked on the side of the highway like it had done so many times before. And if it wasn't out of gas, it suffered from a flat tire, dead battery, or some other illness that left it lifeless next to our trailer.

Another perk of our newest modular home was our luxurious front porch. Sure, it leaned to one side now—the result of a missing concrete cinder block. (We were pretty sure one of our neighbors stole the concrete block and propped up his Oldsmobile to work on it.) Here in Todd's Trailer Garden, a front porch was the equivalent of a nice, green front lawn. A big porch meant we sat outside to barbecue or to enjoy the nice view of filthy, fighting children and hairy, tattooed men.

When we first moved here in August, I enjoyed sitting outside to read or take pictures, but lately I hadn't been outside much. I wasn't in the mood for the constant traffic and drama around Todd's Trailer Garden, and it was too cold anyway. The snow fell like crazy, and the wind bit our uncovered skin like a rabid dog.

When I sat outside, there was no privacy. My *upstanding* neighbors watched me suspiciously, men gawked at me or made cat calls, or women yelled names at me. A person only bent so far before breaking. Like one day, when it was warmer, I sat on our porch completely absorbed in *Wuthering Heights.* One of our neighbors, a thirty-something-year-old, scraggly woman, tripped out of her red dented Dodge Neon and headed towards her mobile mansion. This all happened back when I was still popular and had hair, so most likely my ego was not in check on that day.

Her drunker-than-a-skunk boyfriend followed her out of the car towards the trailer and slurred, "Rose, honey, I didn't meanta call ya that. It just slipped out. You know I've got anger problems. Sometimes I just lose it, but I ain't never gonna do that again. You gotta forgive me this time. You'se as beautiful as any woman in the wurld."

Housewives of Todd's Trailer Garden was right before my eyes. I tried to hide my laughter with my book. The irony of my drunk neighbor's name doubled me over in laughter. She looked more like a withering weed than a rose. This wasn't the first time Rose came home stumbling up the stairs into her trailer, and this wasn't the first boyfriend who followed her up the rickety stairs, begging her forgiveness.

Merl told me to stay inside and lock the door when Rose or one of her boyfriends was around.

"I've got a bad feeling about her," Merl had told me before, one day when we first moved in, as she peeked out the curtains across the driveway. "That woman ain't right."

"Ya think?" I asked. I didn't bother to share any of the other encounters I witnessed in Rose's front yard, while Merl was at work. I didn't want my mom to worry. Funny how quickly my love and aggravation for my mother swung back and forth like a pendulum. Merl meant well, and she loved me and Sammy....in her own way.

I glanced back over the top of *Wuthering Heights.* Rose's boyfriend tripped on her kids' bikes on the way back to the trailer's stairs. The crazy man picked up the bikes, a wagon, and any other toy littered across the yard and threw them into a big pile at the end of the trailer.

"Rose, I ain't tellin' them boys again about leavin' shit all over the yard," he yelled at the closed door.

The incident turned from funny to scary in about two seconds, but this wasn't my first rodeo, so to speak. Rose's boyfriend averted his eyes from the closed door to our front porch where I sat.

"Hey, girlie, what's yur name?" he slurred. "Yur lookin' purty today."

My eyes remained on the book, as if I hadn't heard him. My cell phone sat next to me, but I didn't have any minutes to call anyone and I didn't want the crazy guy to think I was scared. He made it almost across the driveway into our yard, when Rose stepped back out onto her porch.

"Carl! Now where in hell you goin'?" she yelled with her cigarette hanging out of her mouth. A little boy stood behind her, watching the entire escapade.

Carl turned around like a cat caught with a finch in his mouth and walked back to the porch.

"I was cleanin' up the yard, woman," Rose's boyfriend yelled back at her. These people spent half of their days yelling at each other.

"I'm comin' inside now, and you ain't gonna yell no more," the man she called Carl continued. He looked just about like the last boyfriend she called Big Tom with his beer belly and a cutoff T-shirt revealing flabby arms half-white and half-tanned.

This time was different though, because Rose started yelling at me.

"Ya oughta just go inside 'cuz you ain't gonna pick up any of our men out here dressed like a little whore pretendin' to read," Rose yelled at me.

Rose's voice finished with a shriek more irritating than fingernails on a chalkboard. Still trying to find out what Catharine was about to do in my book, it took me a minute to realize Rose was talking to me. I looked up from the book, sat up in my chair, and processed what Rose had just said. My quick temper and wit had gotten me into trouble before, but this time I felt justified in my retort.

"Seriously, you call that a *man*?" I yelled back across the driveway, lifting myself out of the ripped lawn chair. "And I'm not pretending to read, I am reading."

"Sure, ya are," Rose retorted, nearly falling right off the stair. "Ya ain't got nothin' better to do than be nosey and try to see what's a goin' on over here. Little girl, ya best get your nose on yur own face..."

Rose stalled. Carl made it into the trailer finally.

"On yur own face or I'll come over there and abreak it," Rose finished.

Sammy sat inside engrossed in *The Wizard of Oz* for the hundredth time. I was glad he didn't see all of this mayhem outside. At that time, I could have ignored her big mouth and went inside, but my pride didn't allow me to do so. Instead, I yelled back at her, mocking her accent.

"Oh, Rose, dear, you's just jealous *I* can read. And I can tell's you fur sure I ain't wantin' nothin' with your boyfriends. Carl's lookin' like a sasquatch," I finished.

Rose swung her head around and started towards our house. Obscenities rolled off her tongue like vomit. My heart raced. I contemplated an escape route, in case Rose made it to our porch. There was no way, I knew, I'd let her know I was scared of her.

Stay inside, Sammy. Stay inside, Sammy, if she comes over here and beats me to a pulp, I repeated in my head. My next instinct was to pray for Sammy's protection.

Before Rose made it all of the way to our porch, Carl pounced out of the trailer, as if he knew what his girlfriend planned to do.

He grabbed her arm and slurred at her, "Rose, baby, ya need to get back home. She ain't nothin' but a little, mouthy brat. You knows yer still on probation, and ya need to stay outta trouble."

Rose acted like she planned to ignore him, most likely for dramatic effect, and then finally turned back to her trailer. Both of Rose's boys now watched from the front porch. Carl held her by the arm, and the two spun around in a clumsy waltz, as he sweet talked her all of the way back into the trailer.

"That's a good girl, Rose," he muttered.

I smelled alcohol even from my porch.

He continued, "Ya don't wanna mess up yur pretty hair anyway, now do ya?"

Rose stopped and spat on the ground. She hurled one more insult in my direction, "Piss on you, little girl."

My blood boiled again, and I knew she couldn't have the last word.

"Like I said…you're just jealous that I can read," I stated calmly but loud enough for her to hear me. "And you're just jealous I still have all of my teeth."

Promptly, I stood, collected my things, and went into our trailer. Just as I expected, Sammy sat on our couch watching the cowardly lion skip beside the tin man. Promptly, I stood, collected my things, and went into our trailer. Just as I expected, Sammy sat on our couch watching his movie.

The cowardly lion skipped beside the tin man, as the two sang with Dorothy, "Follow the yellow brick road. Follow the yellow brick road. Follow, follow, follow, follow, follow…"

Inside, Sammy sang along, oblivious his big sister barely escaped a brutal beating by Rose the Meth-head. Every time Sammy watched the movie, I wanted to tell him the Wizard of Oz was a phony and the grand wizard wouldn't fulfill ANY of their wishes. Wishes never got answered. But every time I nearly told Sammy the truth, I remembered my baby brother had seen the movie one million times, and he knew the wizard was a fake, but, every time he watched the movie, he cried when Dorothy made it back home. Even if I knew life didn't always work out like you hoped, I couldn't dash Sammy's dreams.

"I guess I oughta just go back inside," I said to myself loud enough for Rose, Carl, and her boys to hear, mocking her redneck dialect. "Somethin' stinks out here anyway."

The old broad had the nerve to flip me off again. Inside, I closed the door, sat beside Sammy, and stole one more peek out of the window to make sure we weren't going to be murdered by Rose. One of our neighbor's, Gwen, stood on her porch, yelling across the driveway at Rose and Carl. Gwen's long fingernails pointed back and forth, as she told them something.

Surprisingly, Rose didn't yell back at Gwen. She and Carl disappeared into the trailer, while Gwen sat on her front porch and smoked a long cigarette and petted a cat. It was obvious our old neighbor wasn't going anywhere. She sat on her porch for another thirty minutes, at least, watching Rose's trailer and our front porch.

The whole encounter with Rose and her new boyfriend scared me a little, but I had lived in enough trailer parks to know you either had to be tough or pretend to be tough in order to survive. Gwen's final showdown with Rose didn't surprise me. From our bus stop, when it was warmer, we all watched Gwen, as she sat on the front porch of her trailer. It was on the other side of our trailer, and Gwen had a clear view of everything that went on.

If there was a *Yard of the Month Award* here at Todd's Garden, Gwen, our sixty-something neighbor, would win it every month. Her stone yard ornaments and solar light collection outnumbered the daffodils and tulips. Everyone knew which trailer was Gwen's, not only because of her landscaping, but also because she was the only resident at Todd's who painted the outside of her trailer.

Every year, they said, Gwen repainted her trailer. This year it was fancy cotton candy pink, single-wide trailer adorned with purple and lime green trim. At first, I thought it was gaudy, but it grew on me. The rumor around the trailer park was Gwen was really a millionaire, and her fortune was buried outside underneath all of those yard gnomes. Rumor had it, her husband, who was now deceased, invented an electrical button or something that enabled push-button phones in the '60's. By the looks of Gwen's trailer, you would've thought, if Gwen had been a millionaire, she already spent all of her winnings on paint, solar lights, and wind chimes. After dark, her trailer looked like a UFO ready to launch.

The legend was before he died, Gwen and her husband lived in a plush mansion in the city, eating at the fanciest restaurants and wearing the best clothes. When Gwen's husband tragically died in a plane crash on his way to a conference, Gwen was institutionalized for some time because of her grief. When she was a little better and allowed to leave the asylum, Gwen moved back into the trailer she and her husband lived in before. Supposedly, Gwen never stepped foot in the mansion again, because it was too painful. A realtor sold the house for her, so that was why she stayed here in our trailer park, since it was where she and her first husband lived before his invention. Gwen never remarried or had children.

Since we moved in, Gwen was always nice to me and Sammy. Actually, she was nice to all of the kids in the trailer park. Gwen never had much to do with the adults, it seemed, but she talked to all of us from time to time. She never mentioned to me the ordeal between Rose and me, but never acted like she was mad at me for mouthing off to Rose either.

As for the legend of Gwen's wealth, I never asked. To me, it didn't matter if the was true or not. She was so good to us, and it didn't matter if she had any money or not. I figured she'd tell me, if she wanted me to know. The only time Gwen even appeared sad whatsoever was around Christmastime. We stopped by her house on Christmas Eve to give her a pan of cookies. Sammy and I made different kinds of cookies to make gift plates for our neighbors we liked. We only had to make three plates.

When Gwen answered the door, she must not have expected any company. Her hair was in curlers, and she had no make-up on. It was the first and only time I'd seen her so natural. She looked so much younger and, in a way, more vulnerable.

"Well, Jett, sweetheart," she said, "I wondered who was knocking on my door. Hi, little Sammy."

"We won't bother you to come in, but we wanted to bring you some cookies," I said.

Gwen didn't mean to be rude, but we could tell she didn't want us to see inside her house.

"Hi, Miss Gwen," Sammy sang in his sweet little voice. "Merry Christmas!"

"Merry Christmas, you little sugar cane," Gwen answered.

Over her shoulder, I saw a tiny Christmas tree and next to the tree, a gorgeous frame with a picture of a smiling man inside of it. Even from the doorway, the man's bright eyes shone. He was handsome. That must have been her husband. He looked so happy.

"Oh, honey, I don't have a lick of makeup on," Gwen answered. "I'd invite you in...."

"No, we have to be getting back," I interrupted.

I didn't want her to feel guilty for not having us come into her house, even though I so badly wanted to ask if that really was her husband and if he really died in a plane crash.

"We have some other cookies to hand out, so we have to get going," I said, which was followed by an awkward pause.

Gwen looked down at the plate of misshapen cookies. Suddenly, I was a little embarrassed at how our cookies looked. We should have taken more time to make sure the cookies looked like a gingerbread man instead of the blob. Gwen saw me eyeing the cookies.

"Wow," she said. "You and Sammy must have spent all day on these delicious cookies."

"No, we used a can of cookie dough, and we just kinda smashed 'em a little," Sammy answered.

I tried to shush Sammy before he said anything else to embarrass me.

"We tried to make them from scratch, but we burned three batches, before giving up," I said.

"Well, next year, you two sweeties will have to come over, and we'll make cookies together," Gwen said, almost like she meant it.

I couldn't tell if she really meant it. Did Gwen even have a kitchen? Would she really like me and Sammy come over and make cookies...like a real grandma? Merl said we planned to move at the end of the school year, so we didn't know if we'd even be here for our next Christmas.

"We don't never see our grandma," Sammy started. "She came a long time ago to see us, but she didn't make no cookies with us. Last Christmas, Grandma came over, but her and Merl got into it, and she left."

I interrupted Sammy again, correcting his grammar, "Any."

"Any what?" he asked.

"Never mind," I finished. Gwen didn't want to hear all about our drama. "We probably should be going now."

Sammy's nose and cheeks were red from standing in the cold. Gwen looked at the two of us and again back down to the cookies.

Her lip quivered as she spoke, "You're the only holiday guests I've had so far."

From what I'd seen across the yard, Gwen never had any guests.

"Well, we love you more than any holiday guest you could ever have," I said, and I hugged her. She smelled of lavender and baby powder.

Another silent pause followed.

Gwen took a deep breath and answered, "I love you too, sweetheart. You, too, Sammy. Thank you again. You better be getting on your way, so you can hand out your cookies."

Gwen didn't know it at the time, but we really did love her. She never knew how we, meaning Sammy, me, and every other kid at the bus stop, looked over at her house every morning when we left and every afternoon when we off the bus. Gwen was there every day. With her car parked in the same place, we knew Gwen watched us from inside, if she wasn't standing on her porch with a faux fur coat and snow boots. Earlier in the school year, when it was warmer, Gwen sat on her porch swing to watch us get on the bus every morning.

She waved and yelled, "Bye, little sweeties."

Most of our parents rarely took the time or made the effort to get out of bed to see us off every morning, but Gwen was always there. Now, with winter settled in, Gwen no longer sat on her porch, waving and watching us depart for school every morning. With the temperatures in the single digits, Gwen sat inside her pretty pink trailer, watching through her trailer's thin window.

From the short distance, we saw her made-up face there every morning. She made sure we all made it on the bus, as she sipped her coffee out of a hot pink mug. As always, Gwen's bleached beehive sat atop her head like a poodle, and her long, magenta nails nearly matched her coffee cup. Even this early in the morning, Gwen's face was animated with blue eye-shadow and thick, black liner surrounding her blue eyes.

Before getting on the bus, every morning, we all turned and waved to her. Every afternoon when we got off the bus, Gwen's was the first face we looked for, and she was there much more often than our parents, watching all of us through the window get off the bus.

During the forty-five minute ride to school, sometimes I passed the time imagining what Gwen's house looked like inside or what Gwen's life was like when she was my age. I envisioned photographing Gwen for an entire art gala when I became a famous photographer. As soon as we moved into Todd's Trailer Garden, Gwen and I hit it off. She motioned me over one afternoon when I was outside picking up trash, and spoke to me as if we were long lost friends. We sat on the porch, never going inside, and talked about everything from favorite books to my childhood.

"Welcome," she began, smiling at me with her bright eyes resembling the cat lounging on her patio table. "You are new to the neighborhood?"

"Yeah," I answered. Getting close to anyone was not in my nature, we usually moved as soon as I got attached to anyone. Merl even woke us up a few different times to move in the middle of the night when we couldn't pay our rent. "...we just got unpacked."

"You are different, my dear," she answered inspecting me closely, seemingly choosing her next words carefully. "I can tell you're not comfortable in a place like this."

Every place I'd ever lived resembled Todd's Garden, so I wasn't sure what she meant. At first, I assumed she may have been a little mental, but as our daily conversations grew longer and longer, I realized, Gwen was anything but crazy. She was uber kind, extremely thoughtful, brilliant, and able to read people like no one else I knew. Intuitive was the word.

Once, while we sat on her porch talking, one of our neighbors, Rose, the same drunk lady who yelled at me before, backed out of her driveway in her red car, running over her son's bike. Rose didn't even stop to see what she ran over, before spinning out on loose gravel.

The two of us watched and shook our heads.

"That lady should lose her license," Gwen said. "She drives like a mad woman."

I laughed and nearly shot soda out of my nose.

"Yeah," I answered. "You should've seen her the other day with one of her boyfriends. They were both smashed, and she got mad at me because her man tried to hit on me. Yuck. He was nasty."

"Oh, that's ridiculous," Gwen muttered, lighting another cigarette and shaking her head. "I'm not even sure how her children make it living with her."

"You saw some of it from here, didn't you?" I asked.

"I most certainly did," Gwen answered. "I heard the whole thing. I laughed for days the way you stood up to Rose. I couldn't have been prouder. When you went inside, I gave Rose and that other drunk a piece of my mind too and told them they better leave you alone, or I'd tell the police about their gardening business."

"Gardening business?" I asked. I wasn't really sure what Gwen meant since Rose didn't have one flower growing in her front yard.

"Oh, never you mind about that," Gwen answered with a sneaky grin. "I got enough dirt on everybody around here, so they won't mess with this old woman."

We continued to watch Rose from Gwen's front porch. She threw her car back into drive, spun more gravel, and propelled the junker towards the road. My camera sat on the patio table in front of me, and I picked it up to click pictures of Rose's tires. My pictures tended to tell pieces of a story. I focused on Gwen's car, which sat silently in front of Gwen's trailer in the same place as the first day we moved in. I took a picture of the long Cadillac. Pollen settled across its hood and trunk, leaving a lime green coat. My camera captured a yellow jacket parked on a thick patch of pollen. I clicked several pictures. Gwen never went anywhere, it seemed. I wondered how she bought groceries.

"Do you ever leave?" I finally asked, laying my camera back down on the table. Gwen didn't seem to mind.

"Not much reason to," she said quietly. "I have most of my things delivered to me. I do a lot of my shopping from QVC or online. Nowhere for me to go. These kids need me here to watch out for them anyway."

"Don't you feel like you're missing something?" I asked. The trailer park had to make a person claustrophobic. This was back when I was naïve and before I learned how dark the outside world could be.

"I don't believe so," Gwen answered, taking a long drag of her cigarette. "I have everything I need right here."

"How long have you lived here?" I asked. It was the closest I came to inquiring of Gwen's past.

"Twelve years, I suppose," Gwen said before changing the subject. "Why that woman is mad. I should call the police on her."

Rose was parked next to the road and yelling at her boys to go back in the house. She finally got back in her car and drove off towards town.

"She better hurry to the bar," Gwen remarked. "She's running late today."

We both laughed and watched Rose's boys continue to play outside alone.

Gwen grew quiet again and added, "Jett, I've found that it's a cruel world out there. There is no protection from what could happen. I'd rather stay here where it's safe and simple. I just pray you never find out how cruel the world can be."

After my hair cut, I often recalled Gwen's last comment and understood what she had tried to tell me.

Gwen and I spent another twenty minutes gossiping about our other neighbors, before I decided to go back home to clean before Merl got off work. As I stood up to leave, Gwen stopped me.

"Jett, you really need to be careful around here," Gwen said thoughtfully.

"What do you mean?" I asked, confused at Gwen's shift in mood again. We were just laughing, and now she looked so serious.

"I've told you before you're different," she continued, "and not everyone will appreciate your touch of class."

"Class?" I laughed. "There's nothing classy about me, except the new chair on our front porch."

I talked Merl into buying the accent piece at the thrift store on a whim. After a three dollar bottle of spray paint, it was beautiful, just as I had imagined it would be.

"No, dear, you may not see it now, but you're going places, and you have something special," she said, squeezing my hand.

That was all before my haircut. I no longer believed her; I was nothing special. Even the on-line massacre of me said so. Gwen only logged into her computer to shop, so she wouldn't understand about how these comments ripped a person into shreds. I knew she wouldn't understand.

But I clung to the time she told me I was special, just in case it had an ounce of truth in it. The thought warmed me every night before I went to bed and even encouraged me to say a prayer that one day I would become something special.

These talks with Gwen became a daily ritual. Sammy and I felt safer knowing Gwen watched us from across the driveway while mom was at work. One day, when it was warmer, Gwen propped a box fan in her door. I peeked through to see what her house looked like on the inside. My camera lens tempted me to zoom up as close as I could get, and I clicked a few pictures when she wasn't looking. The image showed me what Gwen's living room looked like, which was much different than what I'd imagined.

Instead of shiny furniture to match her appearance, the floors were piled high with junk and only one piece of furniture was even visible. An old brown recliner emerged from the piles of trash, obviously where Gwen spent much of her time. The only other noticeable item was a television, covered with bags and dolls and cats. From my angle, it was blurry, but I'd seen enough.

Stuffed animals, porcelain dolls, magazines, clothes, and books...and books and books. Stuff was piled all of the way to the ceiling, leaving nothing but a narrow path. It had to be nearly impossible for Gwen to walk through her living room.

A chorus of unseen cats meowed and hissed inside. There must have been a dozen cats living in all of the junk. Gwen never sat on her porch without Pretty Lady, her favorite cat, nestled in her lap. During our conversations, Gwen stroked the white Angora cat lovingly like a security blanket. Gwen often brought another cat outside with her for me to hold.

Each time it was a different cat. Gwen said she didn't want me to get attached to any particular cat, but I wondered if she was afraid the cats would become attached to me. We couldn't have pets, Merl said, because landlords wouldn't let us, so I pretended Gwen's cats were mine. After the hair incident, Gwen was the only person I told about what was going on at school. I might've told Merl, if she seemed interested in my life. Gwen made a point of making me feel important.

Gwen saw me today run off the bus, just as she did every day. I tried to hide my face to and to make it all of the way to our trailer without looking up, so Gwen wouldn't see my tear-streaked face. I made it all day without crying, but as soon as I took the last step on the bus, I lost it. It turned into one of those cries that hurt your stomach and turned your face puffy and red.

"Are you okay, Jett?" Mike asked me before he opened the door to let all of us off of the bus.

"Yeah, just great," I responded, wiping my eyes quickly. *Hold it in. Keep it all in until you get home,* I repeated to myself.

"Jett, I've seen a change in you," Mike said with his usual southern drawl. "You've got me worried. You know you can talk to me, if you need to."

I turned to look at him from the bottom step and replied, "Thanks, Mike, but I don't think you can help me with this problem."

"Well, just remember the darker it outside, the easier it is to see the stars," he replied.

Mike wasn't only talking about the mean girls at school. He saw where we lived and what went on there on a daily basis. Trash strewn across lawns, adults milling around from trailer to trailer instead of working. It wasn't exactly a great place to grow up. My vast loneliness had turned into depression. No friends. Merl was always at work or with friends. I kept up with school work, took care of Sammy, and kept the house clean.

This most recent turn of events with Neova and Say was just the final letdown for me. I nodded at Mike through my tears and stepped off the bus. *This may be the last time I see him*, I thought. I hoped he wouldn't feel bad tomorrow morning, if I didn't get on the bus. I decided to leave a note for everybody, including him, so he wouldn't feel guilty when I was gone. There was nothing he could say that could've changed my mind.

The plan was to get in Merl's medicine cabinet in her bathroom, where she kept all of her medicine bottles. I planned to take two whole bottles of whatever I found to make sure I fell asleep quickly. I'd put on my favorite outfit, lay down on the couch, and sleep. Gone would be the worries, the pain, and the stress. It would all be gone. Somewhere in between all of that I remembered to write a letter.

To Those I Leave Behind,
Like a Sleeping Beauty...minus the long, beautiful hair,
Here my lifeless body you shall find.
Silently resting, because, for me, life wasn't fair.

I fought the good fight, but, in the end, I lost.
Nothing can save me now—not even a kiss,
For their sins and cruel judgment, my life was the cost.
But those who did me wrong will not even miss.

You all have heard the saying, "If looks could kill."
Well, they have, they do, and they will.
To my loved ones, my last request is for you not to cry for me.
Now here I go … away …as I swallow colorful pills.
Good night. Farewell. Hopefully, one day you all again one day I will see.

-Jett

My plan was to leave the letter on our coffee table underneath Merl's ashtray, to sink into our couch, and to sleep. That would be it. That was my plan, anyway, until Sammy tripped stepping off of the bus. I grabbed his little hands warm in the gloves I made him wear and pulled him up off the freezing, slick ground.

If I left, who would wake my baby brother up in the morning for school? Who would make sure he wore his coat and gloves? And who would pick him up, if he fell down? I was the only constant in Sammy's life, just as he was mine.

As we inched closer to our house, moving slowly over the snow, I saw Gwen's profile cast a shadow through her window. As usual, Gwen watched all of us get off the bus from her trailer. Despite our daily routine, I kept my head down to get Sammy into our house before Gwen stopped us.

I knew she'd wave to me to come over and tell her how my day went. Just as expected, Gwen stepped outside onto her porch, despite the cold, hugging herself in a thick, ancient fur coat.

"Jett," she yelled across the driveway.

Sammy took baby steps, slipping and sliding along the way. I held his arm and helped him up onto our porch and into the trailer.

"Jett, honey, come here," she called again in her honey sweet voice. This wasn't a time to be comforted. I wanted to wallow in my sorrow.

Gwen must have read my mind, and I was ashamed. Part of me wanted to run to her and to tell her everything. Maybe she'd try to talk me out of my plan. The other part of me knew tomorrow and the next day and the next day after that looked as dreary as the last.

"Jett, get over here, little girl," she yelled in a louder voice, "or I'll come drag you over here."

The threat would have frightened me, if it were anybody else. Gwen wouldn't hurt a hair on my head.

"Sammy," I told my little brother through the screen door, "stay in the house. I'll be back in a minute."

Gwen cheerfully waved me over with her long ruby red nails, and I inched in her direction. Old Gwen's nails were a different color every day. She must have repainted her nails, petted her cats, and waited all day for us to arrive home. Good 'ole Gwen didn't miss a thing from her kitchen window like our guardian angel with big bleached hair wrapped in a blue scarf. I fought against the smile, even though I felt so down, just seeing Gwen made me smile. She rarely left her house any farther than her front porch, but her make-up meticulously melted into blue eye shadow and her eyebrows were penciled in beautifully as usual.

"Well, girl, get up here already," she said in her usual shaky voice.

Instead of motioning for me to sit next to her on the snow-covered patio chair, for the first time, Gwen opened the front door. I followed her into her trailer. Every time we'd talked before, we sat on the hard, metal patio chairs. This time was different. I followed her closely, unsure of what I was going to see or why she brought me inside today of all days.

After six months of curiosity, I found what was behind the petite purple door that held so much mystery before. The dining room mirrored her screened porch with a small wooden table and four matching chairs. A cigarette burned in the overflowing, glass ashtray. It appeared she had been sitting there only moments before. A soap opera boomed from the living room television, which sat on a buffet table covered with more dolls.

We walked through her maze of newspapers and dolls. Cabbage Patch dolls, porcelain dolls, Barbie dolls, and dolls I never knew existed were all piled on top of each other. Several towers of dolls reached past my shoulders.

"Don't mind the mess," she said, picking up one of the cats following us along the path. "I meant to pick up a little, but I didn't expect company."

My first reaction was to respond, "Really, Gwen? You haven't had company for months...even years...and you apparently don't pick up, unless you meant to sweep the small path through your kitchen and living room."

Although I was shocked by the mess, I wasn't. As crowded as the small rooms were, they were clean, if that made any sense.

"Wow," I muttered, as I followed Gwen.

"I know, sweetheart," Gwen answered. "My doll collection is amazing, isn't it?"

"Uh, yeah," I answered. Obviously, she misread that cue.

We made our way to the small kitchen table. A cigarette butt burned down to the quick sat in the ashtray and smoke surrounded the duck coffee cup nearby like water vapor emerging from a pond.

"Gwen," I added, still amazed with my old friend's house and still sniffling from the overwhelming feeling of loserdom. I wasn't really sure if loserdom was a word, but if it was, my face would be next to the word's pronunciation in the dictionary.

> **Loserdom**. (lozurdem) *n.* the act of being a loser, or one who never does anything right; one whom everyone thinks is a loser and one whom no one would care if they were swallowed up by weird doll corpses in her neighbor Gwen's trailer house, in which Gwen demonstrates traits of a serious hoarder, which the intruder expected but not at this level.

So, my dictionary entry was much longer than Webster probably preferred, but it was completely accurate. Gwen pulled out one of the chairs for me to sit on. The chair's cushion continued Gwen's cat theme. It appeared to have once been white, but was now stained yellow, most likely from cigarette tar.

"I thought I was gonna have to drag you over here, young lady," Gwen admonished me.

As soon as my bottom hit the cat cushion, I poured out my story. Gwen let me talk the entire time, interjecting "bless your heart" and "those little devils." I told her everything from the night they cut my hair to losing my boyfriend to my best friend. When I finished, a pile of snotty tissues covered the kitchen table. Gwen didn't say anything at first. She didn't tell me that things could be worse or that I shouldn't care what other people said about me.

Gwen reached across the tissue mountain and hugged me.

Her hair smelled sweet like cherries, but with a hint of kitty litter.

"Darling, Jett," Gwen eventually whispered into my ear, "you could shave your entire head, and you'd still be an adorable, little doll."

"Thank you, Gwen," I stuttered through tears, "but I don't feel adorable. I feel horrible and like my world is crashing on top of me."

"Oh, sweetheart," she answered, "you couldn't pay me to go back to those painful teenage years. You just keep on keeping on. You're a strong young lady. Remember how you told that drunk Rose to bug off?"

I nodded. Recalling Rose with her tight jeans and big hair made me laugh.

"Well, you told her right good," Gwen continued. "You aren't scared of anybody or anything. You just keep your head high."

I nodded again. My plan wasn't totally abandoned yet. I left that part out of my story.

Gwen continued, "And if you're hair bothers you that much, what do you think about me fixing your hair? I used to be a hairstylist back in the day."

"I don't think there's anything you could do to make this look better," I said and released the fountain of tears again. "It's not just my hair. My life totally sucks right now."

"Oh, sweetheart," she said, grabbing me into another hug. This time, Gwen cried with me. "Life isn't always fair and doesn't always make sense, but we just have to keep moving forward—one day at a time."

"I don't think I can," I whimpered between sobs.

"You never know how tough you are, until you've finished the fight," Gwen said after a moment.

EMILY

The most exciting thing happened today in Biology class. The teacher told us our final exam this year would be a science project. My mind raced with the multitude of ideas I'd stored in my mind, just in case of an opportunity like this. However, many of my previous ideas did not meet the teacher's requirements. We were given a narrow scope of topics allowed for our project. Finding an acceptable topic would be a project in itself, since the teacher gave us so many guidelines.

Our research proposal was due Monday, and it was supposed to be at least two pages and typed. For the remainder of the day, I spent my other classes focused on the research project. If I had to turn in the research topic by tomorrow, I would only have the weekend to conduct background research and to outline my experiment by Monday. Without a doubt, this was the most fun project of the year.

Playing with my split ends during English class, which was one of my obsessive compulsive habits my counselor asked me to work on, I considered the various experiment possibilities. Mrs. Powell posted our journal entry on the board, and we were supposed to be responding in our notebooks.

The journal entry was, "What could I live without? What could I not live without? In this journal entry, discuss something that may be important to others that is not important to you."

Of course, my mind didn't veer away from the previous class period in which our science teacher had handed us a five-page document outlining our guidelines for the upcoming science experiment. As I continued to brainstorm ideas, I jotted in my notebook, so that Mrs. Powell would not get on to me for being distracted.

> I could not live without watching *Dr. Z: Autopsy Reports* every night at 7:30 p.m. Dr. Z is a coroner in New York, who is given the most challenging autopsies and expected to uncover the causes of death. Dr. Z used advanced evidence from the position of death and other scientific reasoning to determine how a person dies. We were informed that we would be

expected to complete a science experiment as our final project in Biology. I had many ideas, but many of them would have required human hair, which I had trouble obtaining at the time. After I asked another student for her hair, I inquired with local beauty shops, and I still wasn't able to secure the materials necessary to conduct these experiments.

What could I live without? Just about everything that appears to matter to my eighth grade ignoramus counterparts. They are consumed with cell phones and friends, and I didn't understand how they could place so much value in these unimportant items. These girls flip their hair, as if their life depended on their beauty.

Hair follicles.....That was it. Why had it taken me so long to come up with this? I needed to get home as soon as possible to complete the project. I pretended to have a stomach ache, so I could go to the nurse and ask my father to pick me up early from school.

As soon as I got home, I knew what I had to do. I found a pair of sharp scissors in the kitchen and raced into the bathroom, carefully securing a plastic grocery store sack in the sink. I couldn't take a chance at losing any of it down the drain. I began cutting my hair like there was no tomorrow. I couldn't remember my last haircut. The most attention I devoted to my long, auburn hair was to pull it into a bun every morning.

I didn't even take the time to tell my parents my plan to cut my hair. They would understand the importance of acquiring the hair for my experiment. A plastic bag wrapped tightly would store the hair until I began the experiment. In my excitement, I nearly forgot I needed to study before Dr. Z came on.

NEOVA

Say repeatedly told me I shouldn't feel bad about what we did to Jett. I wanted so badly to turn back time and un-do what we had done. What we did was wrong, and I knew no matter how many times Say tried to convince me otherwise. Every time I saw Jett at school or on the bus, I felt worse and worse. Jett looked so deflated like a balloon without air. The confident, creative girl I met last summer was gone, leaving an empty shell of a girl who wore oversized hoodies, short black and pink hair, and hollowed eyes. What we'd done wasn't only about screwing up her hair; we destroyed her.

Daily, when I saw her, I fought the urge to run up to her and to apologize. But I didn't. Part of me was scared of what Say would do to me if I didn't go along with her and part of me was scared of what Jett would say to me. Every day, I stood beside my cruel "friend," joining in the rude comments when Jett walked by. I knew Jett never would have taken the verbal abuse before, but she no longer was Jett. She walked through the hallways like a ghost, as if she were so faint you weren't sure if she was really there or not.

One time when Jett passed our lockers, Say noticed my guilty conscience and her joking mood morphed into anger.

"Quit staring at her like she didn't deserve it," Say sneered at me. "She asked for it."

"What?" I asked. "I didn't say anything."

"You didn't have to," she responded. "You better hope she doesn't tell anyone what we did, or we'll *all* be in trouble. If we get caught, you know, they will send me off somewhere. Do you even care?"

Say stressed the word *all*, slammed her locker shut, and stormed off to her next class. Say flipped out a lot lately. She was edgier than usual, and I figured it was a combination of worrying over Jett ratting us out and her not knowing where she would be moved to next. A caseworker informed Say she would be relocated to another foster home soon and that if she got into any more trouble, they would place her in a juvenile detention facility.

From what Say told me before, being moved in with another foster family was like playing Russian roulette. Part of me felt sorry for Say. No kid should have to live with the unknown of where you would live next. This would be Say's tenth move in four years, since her mom went to prison. Say never told me what her mother did, but I knew Say didn't expect her to be out any time soon.

My friend shared very little about her past, but rarely she would remark about a house she lived in with her mom or tell a dramatic story about a depressing holiday. According to Say, every home she'd been in was hellish. Since our incident with Jett, I no longer felt sorry for Say. My view shifted. She was a victim of misfortune and bad circumstances. But why would she want to put anyone else through so much?

I knew the answer. Say didn't like sharing me. She saw Jett as a threat. I was Say's property, and Jett unknowingly had trespassed. It was my fault this happened to Jett.

I met Jett when she first moved here to Jefferson County. It was a few weeks before school started. Our apartment complex was right behind Todd's Trailer Garden, where Jett lived, and I sat on our back balcony while she moved in her stuff. All incognito, I watched she, her little brother, and mother moved in all of their bags. She looked pretty nice, and the next day I walked over to meet her.

We hit it off and talked for hours about the different books we liked to read. She told me about her old schools and how she was tired of moving. We seemed to have a lot in common. We both lived with single moms who worked all of the time. We both dreamed of having huge careers. I would be a famous hairdresser, and Jett dreamed of becoming a famous photographer and traveling the world. We both detested talk shows and loved sun-bathing. We both loved gummy bears and cherry soda. We were inseparable for the next two weeks until school started.

At first, I didn't introduce Jett to Say. I didn't want to share my new friend, and I didn't really see Say much during the summer. She lived closer to town in a quaint suburb with her foster parents and two other foster kids. Jett and I had a different kind of connection than I had with Say. With Say, my face was forced into an emotionless blank slate.

It was so nice to have a friend right in my backyard. Jett and I sat, flipped through magazines, made fun of Jett's neighbors, or scoped out Flick'r on her mom's laptop. From the beginning, we clicked, and I thought we were true friends. When school started, though, things changed.

Jett wasn't at our bus stop on the first day of school, which was strange, but I saw she got on the bus at a nicer neighborhood. I planned to ask her about it at school, but by the time I saw Jett again, she was with Chloe and other popular girls. One of the first things I told Jett about Jefferson Junior High was to beware of Chloe. She tormented and bullied me every year since third grade. I just didn't see how Jett and Chloe had so much in common. After three days of school and being ignored every freakin' time I saw Jett, I got the point. She wanted to be fake and popular rather than be real and be my friend. Jett made it clear I wasn't cool enough for her.

BILLY

Today ain't been a good day a'tall. I felt like Alexander in that book called something like *Very Bad, Horrible Day.* Everything was goin' along pretty good when I was ridin' the bus there and messin' with my friends, but once I got to school, it all went down the drain. I forgot my library book at home, so the 'ole teacher hollered me and pulled my stick.

Then I didn't get no recess all day just 'cause of the puled stick and she gave me a dumb book I don't never plan to read anyways. Then later our teacher gave us this math quiz for us to go as fast as we could addin' and subtractin'. I forgot everything I done knowed and just wrote a bunch of numbers down as fast as I could.

After the quiz, the teacher called me back in the hallway and told me to quit messin' 'round and start usin' my head. By the time we got to lunch, I was just about a nervous wreck. The fat cook with hairy arms done handed me a tray, when this boy outta nowhere boy bumped into me 'causin my hotdog to shoot plum out of its bun like a torpedo. My coleslaw plopped straight down on my foot and my chocolate pudding landed right smack dab on my pants. It looked like I done gone and pooped myself.

When I went to sit down, everbody laughed at me. Since we get free lunches, the lady said I don't get another tray, and I hadta just go without. My stomach growled like a hound dog the rest of the day, and everybody called me poopy pants 'cause when I went to wipe the pudding off my crotch, it just smeared it, makin' a bigger browner spot.

The nurse let me try to call home, but Cheryl's phone was turned off and the only pants the nurse got for me to borrow looked like girly pants. I walked around the last hour of the day with purple and pink polka dot pants two sizes too little. It hurt to walk or even bend over in them ugly pants. The dumb pants even gave me a rash on my butt.

When I finally made it home, Cheryl said she made somethin' new for dinner, so I knew that my day wasn't gonna get no better. I barely swallered down half the tuna slop casserole the dumb broad made and puked in my mouth a little tryin' to do that. As soon as I could, I took off outside to my tree house. Since it was so darned cold, I didn't go out there as much as in summertime. That night, I no more cared about the freezin' cold than the man on the moon.

I hadta be alone to catch my breath. I wanted to hit stuff with my hammer and break stuff. Dad said I was just like him and had ADHL, or something like that, but I just don't like people much. Dandy, my beagle, stayed out in his house near my tree house, so I sat out there and talked to him mostly. I couldn't really call my tree house a real tree house though…not like the ones on TV. It was just a cardboard box a refrigerator came out that I drew on and put outside under a tree.

It was one thing that was all mine and where I kept my hidden food. Every Friday our teacher gave some of us a plastic bag of food like peanut butter, crackers, cans of soup, and such. We all knew who got them bags of food 'cause it was the same people. Everbody at Todd's Trailer Park got one for sure. Cheryl didn't never even know about my bag 'cause knowin' her she'd steal it straight from me like a thief and use it to feed everbody.

I kept all of this food hidden since Cheryl made sure we got nothin' but tiny scoops of food on our plates, and a growin' boy needed more than that to grow, so I hid out in my treehouse and scarfed my snacks. Cheryl thought she was so smart sittin' all day, watchin' talk shows and decidin' what to order from Avon. She wasn't smart at all. She was a dumb broad, and she ain't got no clue I outsmarted her with my hidden food. Since I dropped my food on my lap today at lunch and then 'bout puked on her nasty tuna casserole, I knew I earned some extras.

That danged Cheryl tried tellin' us her tuna recipe was straight from Rachel Ray, and it was "gonna be tantalizin". She's nothin' but a liar, and when I smelled that tuna as soon as I stepped off the bus, I was aknowin' we were in fer it.

The next day of school was gonna be Friday anyway, and they gave us another bag of stuff. After five minutes in my treehouse and three packages of peanut butter crackers and four beef jerkies, I knew I best be gettin' back inside cause it was so darned cold.

Tomorrow was gonna havta be a better day than today. I was gonna hold on to my lunch tray extra hard, makin' sure nobody's 'round to bump into me when I got it. And it was gonna be the best day of the week. Every Friday we watched a movie and gotta eat bunches of popcorn and drank fruit juice 'til our whole lips and tongue turned red and burned from too much salt.

MRS. POWELL

Jett didn't show up to class yesterday, which concerned me after reading her journal entry. Today she did, though, thank goodness. She walked right into class and hid in the back desk, a different young lady than before Christmas break. She looked like a lost puppy without her normal confident stride and quick remarks. Whereas Jett once participated in class, now she barely made eye contact with anyone anymore. I watched to see if there was a change in her circle of friends. Sadly, Jett appeared to no longer have any friends. She walked from my classroom straight to her locker and then straight to her next class, without saying a word to anyone.

I also noticed the change in Jett's appearance. Her hair, which was long and beautiful, was nearly shaved off. She wore clothes three sizes too big. I wondered if this had something to do with the lack of friends now. With kids, nowadays, it was hard to tell if this was a fashion statement, but it seemed to have worked against Jett.

I needed to speak with Jett to see what was going on. After my years of teaching, I knew timing was everything with these children. I decided to take a more indirect approach with Jett and assigned the entire class the following journal entry: "What could I live without? What could I not live without? In this journal entry, discuss something that may be important to others that is not important to you."

I hoped Jett's responses, as well as some of my other students' entries, would help me gain insight into what was going on. My first notion was Jett's problem was here at school, but I didn't doubt there was more to it. Jett wasn't from the best upbringing, which I certainly related to. I saw a little of myself in Jett. My husband didn't exactly have the best raising either, so I knew I was attracted to others who hadn't been dealt the upper hand. Although we never talked about his childhood, we grew up together and I knew he had an awful childhood. I overheard my parents talk about his mother and father, when they thought I was asleep.

They said his dad was "*nothin' but a drunken sailor spendin' his life at sea or in the local tavern*" or "*it's a cryin' shame that boy has to grow up in that mess and his mama just shows up at church with a black eye and everything.*"

Funny how, even now, after thirty years of marriage, we still never talked about his dad. I supposed it was me who never brought it up, but I didn't think he would want to think about it. He's been through so much. You couldn't tell it all by looking at him. He was forever smiling and cutting up. That's one of the main reasons I married him. My husband made me laugh.

CHLOE

Have I mentioned how dumb my parents are?! They caught me texting at nine o'clock last night when I was supposed to be doing my homework, and you would have thought I stole money from their 401K accounts. They took turns preaching at me about the importance of good grades and good jobs and whatever else they thought of saying to me. When they tag-teamed me with these lectures, I thought they half-way enjoyed it since it was one of the few things they did together. They probably even planned it out beforehand.

My father said to my mother, "Hey, honey bunny, instead of taking a date night to go out for dinner and movie, maybe we can catch our little Chloe doing something wrong and have a 30-minute lecture instead?"

My mother, who was well-known for her lengthy, grueling closing statements, grabbed his arm with a big smile on her face, "Oh, babe that sounds like a great evening together, especially since we haven't seen each other in like a week. That would be the perfect way to spend our family time together. Let's go find our daughter and get started. Hopefully, she is doing something terribly horrific, so that our lecture can take three hours."

Sickening. I knew this fantasy wasn't true, since my father and mother never spoke to each other that nicely any more. So, my mom returned to my bedroom upstairs again around ten o'clock to tuck me in, as if she and my father hadn't just spent thirty minutes lecturing me. She pretended to be a good mother, even though I wasn't two years old. She explained how she was working on some big case, as usual, which was why I hadn't seen her in two days. In her insincere, sappy, mother-of-the-year voice she tried to ask me how school was.

"Same as always," I replied. "Dull and a waste of time."

"Now, come on," mom answered. "There has to be something exciting going on?"

"Oh, yeah, watching Mr. Guffman's nasty, green armpits during class was so freakin' exciting," I answered without giving her the pleasure of eye contact.

My fingers continued their routine of texting back and forth with Keagan and my new best friend, Molly, on my cell phone. My parents were so stupid. After their lecture earlier, they handed me back my phone. They never followed through with anything, not even their punishments.

I could have told her about our history teacher, Mr. Guffman, a.k.a. Green Armpit Man, who sweated profusely throughout his lessons. Supposedly, our history teacher was known to have secret dates with high school girls—ugly ones—and thought he was quite the lady's man. Every day in class, he strutted around like a rooster with his spiked red hair, talking non-stop and pausing only long enough to push a button on his computer to move his Power Point forward or to take a long gulp of bottled water. Some days he actually wiped sweat from his face with a towel, as if he were finishing a workout. What a freak.

Today, Mr. Guffman became increasingly passionate, waving his arms around as he walked up and down the row of desks. He explained emphatically how the Cold War impacted our country and how kids in the '50's learned to climb under their desks in case of a nuclear fall-out. As hard as Mr. Guffman tried to keep our attention, the only falling outs we were all really paying attention to were the green clumps of deodorant Mr. Guffman fired out of his green, hairy armpits. A big chunk fell in front of me in the floor. I kicked it out of the way, clearly disgusted, but it stuck to my shoe.

So, I knew it was nasty, but in order to maintain the attention I was getting from the two boys next to me, I was dramatically trying to get it off of me.

"Oh yuck," I squealed when Mr. G's back was turned. "This is soo nasty!"

One of the boys pretended he was going to wipe it on me, so I bounced in my chair, flipping my perfect hair. Another green clump fell right in front of Jett.

She reacted before thinking and said, "It looks like something Neova would wear as eyeshadow."

If Jett had made the comment before Christmas break, the class would have roared with laughter, but now Jett wasn't allowed to be funny. A few of the boys still laughed and pointed at Neova, who endured our nasty comments so often. Jett knew the mistake she made as soon as the words came out of her mouth.

"More like something that came out of your hair," I said, looking up at her jacked up hair.

My comment received the laughter I expected. Mr. Guffman barely noticed his students weren't listening or that Jett got up and ran out of the classroom.

Of course, when my mother asked about school, I didn't share with her this entire story. She didn't need to know about my personal life. It was none of her business. If she was so worried about it, she wouldn't be gone for days at a time and she wouldn't zone out when I decided to humor her and answer her stupid questions.

"Well, it sounds like at least you are paying attention in class," my mother responded, and that was it. That was the extent of our deep conversation for the day. She bent down to kiss me goodnight. The familiar smell of sweet vanilla lotion tempted me to throw my arms around my mom's neck and hug her back. But instead I arched my back away from her and moved my face towards my phone again, so she couldn't kiss my forehead.

As my mom started to turn the knob to leave, she stopped and said, "Chloe, I know I have been working a lot lately, but I will make this up to you. When we finish this case, we'll take a little road trip...just you and me. How does that sound?"

This wasn't the first time I had heard these false promises. I knew by now once one "big case" was closed, there would be another case just as important. My mother couldn't just pass up a huge opportunity to make a tally mark in her column of wins. I also knew one of my mom's major goals was to be tapped as a partner at her law firm and to earn this promotion, she had to continue winning cases.

"Oh, just fabulous," I responded with the sarcasm seeping like sap from a tree. "I'm sure it will be just a splendid time, mother, two years from now when you finally have the time to go on this fabulous road trip."

I added the last dig just to make sure I hurt her feelings in case the first part of my smart aleck remark didn't do the trick. I was out-of-line with my mom, but to me, what was really out-of-line is seeing your *only* child every three days, while the "said daughter" paces through an empty house bored out of her mind.

My mom paused one last time before leaving my room.

"You know I love you more than anything, Chloe," she said in a hushed voice. "You're still my little sugar plum. I'm sorry I haven't been around enough lately. I promise I really will make it up to you this time."

"Yeah, mom, whatever, good night," I said, continuing to fire texts to my friends about my mom annoying me.

Once she was gone and my door was closed again, I wiped away the lone tear trickling down my cheek. My heart hurt from being so mean to my mom, but I knew I wouldn't get out of bed and go downstairs to apologize. I knew deep down I'd love to take that road trip.

FRIDAY

JETT

Although I knew today would be as pathetic as every other day since Christmas break, I forced myself to go to school. I woke up Sammy. My current life was pathetic, but poor Sammy's life was extremely uneventful. He didn't appear to be bored. Melancholy was a vocabulary word in Mrs. Powell's class last week. I loved the word. Melancholy was a word Sammy never understood.

He was content ever since the day he was born. No matter where or how we had lived over the years, Sammy never complained. The last time we went a week without electricity, waiting for Merl to earn enough tips to get it turned back on, I pouted. Sammy was able to bring me out of the dumps. He convinced me to pretend we were camping and to make the best of it.

At our last trailer, there was one bedroom, which of course was Merl's. Sammy and I shared the couch in the living room. He had to be uncomfortable, but he never said a word about it. When I asked him if he wished he had a bed to sleep in, he said he was just glad he got to sleep with me and that's all he cared about. Sammy said he didn't get scared as long as he slept with me, and he liked my stories. As we cuddled on the plaid couch, squashed in between scratchy cushions, I recited the stories of Hercules and Perseus from memory.

"One day, you'll be big and tough just like Hercules and Perseus," I told him.

"I'll go on trips and slay monsters," Sammy answered.

"Yep, if you want," I answered. "You can do anything you put your mind to."

"I'd be way too scared to go on a trip by myself like them," Sammy added. "They must be really brave to go all over the world even in the dark."

""No, you wouldn't," I answered groggily, half-awake. "You have a heart of gold, and you wouldn't be scared of anything. You're tougher than me, Sammy. They were much older than you are, so you have a while before you have to be that brave."

"One day I'll be brave like them," Sammy yawned.

"I know you will," I answered. "I love you, bubby."

Sammy was fast asleep before he could respond.

Part of Sammy's ability to be content was his wild imagination. He had invisible friends to keep him company. Once in a while, I let my little brother play with the other boys in our trailer park, like Billy, the little boy who was always dirty. I only let him though when I could watch them the entire time. Now that it was too cold for him to play outside, he had to spend all of his free time inside with me. When mom worked late, I heard him in his bedroom talking to his friends, Cocoa, Schimley, and, who else other than, Batman. I told Merl about his imaginary friends just to make sure she didn't think it was too strange. She said he would grow out of it eventually.

When I went into Sammy's bedroom to wake him up, he was laying just as I expected. He was snuggled up with RaRa and fast asleep. I nudged him awake, reminding him it was Friday. Friday meant we had all weekend to stay home watching movies or reading. Friday also was mom's big money day. Merl worked doubles every Friday, and the restaurant had much more business on the weekend. Every Saturday morning, we awoke to the jingles of mom counting change she earned the night before in tips. Weekends were best when Merl was between boyfriends, because it was time with her alone. Every Saturday morning mom sat at the table with a nervous grin, piling up dollar bills and quarters at the kitchen table, hoping it would be enough to cover all of the bills for the month.

We joined Merl, ate Cheerios, and heard the latest gossip from the restaurant. Cheryl, Billy's step-mom a lady, applied at the restaurant this week and cussed out the boss, when he told her she needed to clip her fingernails, if she was going to be a waitress.

Merl reenacted Cheryl's response, "Now, ain't nobody nowhere gonna tell me what to do with my nails...or my hair for that matter. I take a lot of time makin' myself look this beautiful, and I ain't needin' this job bad enough to clip my nails."

We spent nearly the entire morning every Saturday with Merl, and she gave us her undivided attention, for the most part. Merl asked us about school and told us about how she talked sweet to old men at the restaurant to score big tips.

"Compliment men, Jett," our mother taught me. "It don't matter how old, young, tall, or short, men like someone talkin' sweet to 'em and tellin' 'em what they wanna hear."

I added this advice to my arsenal to become popular. They weren't old men at school I flattered, but it worked, nonetheless. The more I complimented the popular girls, and even boys for that matter, the more they included me.

Weekends were the best, especially if Merl had a really good night of tips. After breakfast, she took us shopping to get a new shirt or some groceries. Sammy and I crossed our fingers while Merl counted her tips, hoping she raked in the cash, so we could go shopping. We usually went to the second-hand stores, but I knew to look for name-brand clothes resembling the cool kids at school. I did the same for Sammy, even though he didn't really care about clothes.

Sammy and I got ready for school, guessing how much Merl would bring home from the diner, and rushed to the bus stop. Before we left, Sammy asked if he could take Ra-Ra to school. It was hard to tell Sammy no. He batted his eyelashes, as he explained about movie day, and his class was allowed to wear pajamas and bring stuffed animals.

I threw a few bags of cheese puffs and a pack of cookies from the cabinet into his backpack, just in case they were supposed to bring snacks for the movie. Mom was gone, but I knew she wouldn't care since our food allowance would be in soon. We trekked along a thin layer of snow towards the bus stop. Snow meant one of two things. Merl came home with big tips, because customers didn't want to cook, or

Merl came home with no tips, because they were too scared to drive to the restaurant.

The snow coming down was thin and flaky like cotton candy. Sammy held his head back, stuck his tongue out, and captured as much as he could.

"Sis, can we make snow ice cream tomorrow?" he asked.

"I guess," I answered, pretending to be annoyed. Sammy knew I loved playing in snow as much as he did. It crossed my mind again how I nearly left my baby brother last night.

The snow was turning into small chunks of ice.

"Ouch," Sammy said. "They're getting harder."

"Yeah, I'm not really sure we'll be able to use ice for our snack," I said. "We can always make snow cones though."

The ground was becoming slick, so I was glad I made Sammy wear his snow boots. On the news last night, the weatherman warned us there was an eighty-percent chance of snow flurries and accumulation. I layered clothes to stay warm and to disappear. I no longer took time to pick out an outfit to impress my friends, since I no longer had any. One more Friday down.

Only fourteen more until school was out. Merl mentioned last week we may be moving over the summer. I told her I'd love to move again. I didn't tell her why, because I knew she had enough to worry about. If we moved, I knew, I'd get to start over one more time. Running away seemed much easier than moving on to high school next year and enduring another year like this one. My hair would be grown out.

• • •

After the three o'clock bell rang, I ran out to the bus as quickly as possible, as I did every day, dodging eye contact and rude comments along the way. The ground was more covered than it was before school, and it came down hard. I slipped several times on the sidewalk. My tennis shoes weren't the best choice for the weather. Sammy was already sitting in the front of the bus, waiting for me to join him with his bright eyes.

Our bus went by the elementary school first, in the afternoons, and then picked us up at the junior high. Sammy didn't know why I didn't sit with Chloe anymore. He didn't seem to care, since I sat with him near the front of the bus now. After climbing over him to stare out the window, I counted down the minutes until the bus engine roared, and we left.

"Hey, Jett," Mr. Mike said, looking back over his shoulder. He wore his usual cowboy hat. Once in a while he switched it up and wore his DAV ball camp. "TGIF, huh?"

"You have no idea," I answered. I couldn't help but smile back at him.

"You havin' a better day?" he asked.

"I guess," I answered. "Another day down."

The sadness hadn't completely evaporated and probably never would.

"Well, I'll get you home as soon as I can," he chuckled back. Just after the last student boarded, Mike closed the bus door. Before shifting into drive, Mike turned around to look at me in one of the front seats.

"You'll make it, kid," he said seriously. It was one of the few times I'd seen our driver without a smile. "I got faith in 'ya. You're a fighter."

My eyes filled. He wasn't the only one who told me that.

"Thanks, Mr. Mike, that really does mean a lot to me," I answered, wiping my face. I looked quickly out the window, so no one saw me cry. I glanced up just in time to meet eyes for a quick moment with none other than Chloe.

Why was Chloe on the bus anyway? She was slumming it. Chloe usually rode with her parents. Ha, ha, Chloe, you're stuck with the losers! Of course, this was part of my internal dialogue that never made it out of my lips. The bus moved out of the parking lot with a growl.

Out of the bus window, the snowflakes accumulated on the ground below. The ground was an Etch-A-Sketch, in my mind, and I wrote my name in cursive. I pulled my camera out of my backpack, turned the flash off, and took pictures out the window. The thick, white snow reminded me of the night before.

After leaving Gwen's trailer, I made dinner for Sammy and put in his favorite movie. Merl worked the late shift, so I used her bathroom to take a long, hot bath. Once in the tub, I couldn't decide if I was going to finish my plan. Merl's razor sat next to the shampoo. So easily, I could have taken it to my wrists. I picked the razor up and traced a my veins up my arm, leaving a thin line of red blood. I lifted my camera off of the floor next to the tub, careful not to get water on it. I took a picture of my wrist, and a picture of my pink toe nail.

Death or life? I saw the two images in black frames in an art gallery. Eight thick zigzagged lines, and it would have been over. And over would be my pictures, Sammy's happiness, and me. When I got out of the bath, I knew cutting my wrists was too cliche anyway. An artist needed to select a more original way of dying. I pulled on Merl's robe, and opened her medicine cabinet, which was decorated with pill bottles, toothpaste, and make-up. A coffee cup from the back of the toilet left by Merl earlier that morning became the pill holder. Her pink lipstick left rings around the mug's rim. After pouring several bottles into the coffee cup, I counted them. Twelve blue capsules, nine oval peach pills, and three fat white ones. The names all sounded like another language. A few bottles looked to be expired. That didn't matter, since they were supposed to do me in. Looking up the names of the medicine online would have played games with my head, so I chose not to learn my killers' identities. Before I could talk myself out of it, I put the coffee cup to my lips and began to tilt my head back. Just as my filled with plastic capsules, Sammy sang out from the living room along with his favorite movie. His angelic voice floated through the bathroom door.

In perfect tune with Dorothy, Sammy sang so innocently and so honestly, "Somewhere over the rainbow, skies are blue....."

The door blocked my view of Sammy, but he most often watched the movie from the couch with his feet propped on the coffee table. His followed Dorothy across the screen intently. Sometimes, he even stood and mimicked her moves, as he sang with her. Before I swallowed, I saw Sammy finding me on the couch asleep and his devastated face as I cried for help. Before I spat them out, one pill slid down my throat and I shot the rest into the sink. Merl's favorite blue high heels became my new weapon, as I hammered all over the pills. I hit. I slammed. I threw stuff. And I hit more.

It felt so good to release. Powder and empty capsules shot all over the bathroom sink, but I couldn't stop there. The heels found Merl's makeup bag, which became their next victim. As angry tears cut down my face, the heels hammered and slammed and destroyed some more.

"Sis?" Sammy said, knocking on the door. The sound of breaking glass must have interrupted his song.

"Sis? You okay? Did you fall?" he asked. He sounded scared.

"No, bubby, I'm alright," I said, forcing back the quiver in my voice.

"Can I come in?" he asked.

My poor bubby stood on the other side of the door scared to death. Merl's bathroom sink looked like a tie dye shirt. Colorful pill powders, smashed chunks of lipsticks, and blurred black mascara contrasted the white porcelain sink. Merl was going to kill me.

"No, bub," I said. "I'm almost done, and I'll be out. Go back and finish your movie. Okay?"

"Alright," he answered hesitantly, "but you yell for me, if you need me, okay?"

My camera begged for me to capture this moment of insanity. I shot pictures of the sink and the evidence of how close I came to insanity. A nanosecond would have been enough time for me to swallow a cupful of pills and end it all, but I couldn't do it to Sammy.

A toothbrush helped me gag up the pill I accidentally swallowed, or at least some of it.

"Sis? Are you throwing up?" Sammy asked. His voice became more urgent. "If you don't come out soon, I'm going to call Merl at the diner. You may need to go to the hospital."

"No, bubs," I answered, wiping tears from my face. Suddenly, I was exhausted. "I'm fine. Don't you worry. You go and turn your movie back on and sing to me some more. I had a little stomach ache, but I'm all better now."

I chose to give myself one more day. After we spent the morning Saturday with Merl, I decided to try again, so Merl would find me and not Sammy.

All of these thoughts swirled through my head like the snow outside of the bus window, as Mr. Mike drove us home Friday afternoon. The snowflakes scattering on tree branches, the ground, and other cards reminded me of flying pill powder.

We were one of the last ones to get home every night, so it was a long ride. Mike usually spent most of his bus route singing along to country music on his radio. Seeing him in front of me with tufts of gray hair poking out underneath his worn hat, I felt a sadness thinking about my funeral. Would Mike attend? How would Merl pay for it all? Hopefully, she wouldn't pick out a fancy coffin. The only joy in thinking about my funeral was hoping Say and Neova felt horrific guilt for what they did to me. Chloe would feel like dirt for how she rejected me after my haircut. Keagan would admit to the congregation that he never stopped loving me.

Mike's voice awakened me from the daydream. He wasn't listening to his radio. Mike spoke to someone at the school's transportation office.

"Doggone it, they should've called school off today," Mike said in an unusually irritable tone. "I'm goin' as slow as I can, and I'm still slidin' all over the place."

I sat straight up in my seat and listened closer to what he said on the radio. The other little kids sat around me oblivious. They were too busy eating their pencil erasers or their boogers. Most of the older kids in the back of the bus were just as clueless. In between flirting and playing with their cell phones, they didn't have time to be aware of their surroundings.

"I'm goin' to try to keep goin', but if it gets any worse, I'm pulling over," Mike told whoever was on the other side of the radio. "How are the other drivers doing out here?"

The only other two on the bus who seemed to be notice Mike was concerned were Emily, the weirdo who asked for my hair one day in the cafeteria, and Daniel, a quiet, mysterious eighth grader. Emily sat in the front too to avoid the jerks in the back. She watched Mike, wrote in her notebook, and glanced nervously out the window.

Daniel sat in the back seat, staring out his window. His bright hazel eyes met mine for a brief second, and my heart raced. He looked worried. From across bus seats filled with immature, stinky kids, we'd made an unspoken connection for the first time. I'd seen him for months getting on and off of the bus, but I'd never really looked at him.

His long, dark eyelashes were partly covered by dark brown bangs, attempting to hide his eyes. As usual, the wires from his earbuds hung down into his brown leather coat collar. My camera lay in my bag, begging me to take his picture, but I knew that would be too weird. The flash would give me away. I looked back at Mr. Mike, sensing his worry.

Our bus crawled forward through the sleet, as its windshield wipers struggled to keep a peep-hole clear for Mike to see the road.

"I can barely see anything," Mike muttered to himself. "I'm gonna have to pull over and wait it out."

Mike wasn't himself at all. I'd never heard him raise his voice ever.

"Hey, guys, I need ya'll to quiet down please," Mike finally yelled at all of us on the bus. It by far wasn't a mean yell, but nonetheless, it was the first time Mike had yelled at us, so everyone jumped into attention.

The bus went quiet. All of the kids left on the bus faced the front silently. Normally, on the way home from school, Sammy talked my ear off about the cool things he'd done at school or about how his friend, Buddy, slung paint into a classmate's hair. Today, he had been quiet the entire way, and I knew he must have felt the tension from Mr. Mike and me.

"Sis," he whispered, moving only his lips, "what's going on?"

Once we were closer to our stop at the trailer park, I finally allowed myself to relax. More than half of the kids had been safely dropped off. I moved my hands from the top of the bus seat in front of me and noticed my knuckles were as purple as Mike's.

Sweat stains remained smeared on the plastic seat in front of me. I took snap shots in my mind of the delicate snowflakes that continued to dance outside my window. Mike's radio sputtered uneasy static and fell quiet.

Mike muttered under his breath, "The dern thing died again."

Before leaving city limits, we'd passed several wrecks. Abandoned cars were sprinkled along ditches like ice-covered tombstones. Getting seven miles down the road took at least forty-five minutes, since Mike could barely see the road. Now the road was more isolated, and no cars passed us. Although everything was covered in snow, the road in front of us was more visible. Sammy sat next to me with his red stocking cap pulled down over his ears about to fall asleep. His little lips were chapped as bright as the cap, so I dug through my bag to find lip balm to put on them.

A packrat by nature, it took me a minute to wade through gum, markers, and other miscellaneous junk I carried in my a huge bag. Everywhere I went, I carried an exuberant amount of items, which was a habit from moving all the time. Any moment Merl could tell us it was time to move again, so I was prepared. I covered Sammy's lips with lip balm. When I looked back up at Mike and into his rearview mirror, I saw a car followed us.

"She better get off my tail end," Mike said to himself.

The car acted like it was going to try to pass the bus. It moved around a couple of inches, but stalled to get back behind the bus.

"What is tarnation is that lady doing?" Mike muttered.

When the red car made its attempt to pass, I got a better look at the car, and I immediately knew why it looked so familiar. Just as the car got behind the bus again, the driver cut it sharp and bumped our side.

"What the heck?" Mike said. He slammed on the brakes before the car hit us again, sending the bus into a spiral across the icy road. Screams erupted throughout the bus, as we all realized the bus was out of control. Mr. Mike held the steering wheel, trying to maintain control, but the road conditions gave him no traction.

His rearview mirror reflected the image of the junky red car. She stopped briefly and then sped around us, as the bus continued to slide, eventually hitting the frozen guardrail. Busting through, the bus snagged, hanging on to both broken steel guardrails.

When I looked behind us, the car was no longer there, but she stopped her car less than half a mile up in front of us. She had to have seen the bus lodged in the guardrail. The bus teetered, and the children's screaming stalled momentarily when the bus came to a halt. Every move they made inched the bus closer to a face-first fall down the icy hillside.

"Don't move!" Mike yelled from his perch at the front of the bus.

No one moved and the bus became silent momentarily.

"Everybody to the back now," Mike yelled. He sat back down stoically in the driver's seat. "Stay calm but move slowly towards the back emergency exit. Now."

Some of the children continued to cry, but they were no longer screaming. The guardrail was all that stood between our bus and a spine-chilling drop. We were stuck. As Mike moved cautiously to pull the parking brake, one at a time, several children tiptoed towards the back.

"Daniel," Mike called, watching him in his rearview mirror.

"Yes, sir," Daniel yelled back, standing erectly like a soldier from one of the back seats.

"When I tell you to," Mike continued, "open the back emergency door and start helping the kids jump out. It looks like there will be a small jump, but everyone should be fine. Everyone needs to look both ways for traffic and then run across to the ditch on the other side of the road."

"Sounds good," Daniel answered. His face appeared to be calm, but his voice shook when he answered.

"Okay, guys, come on," Mike yelled loud enough for the children to hear. "Everybody get to the back and do what Daniel says. I'll come back once you're all moved."

One by one, the children in the middle tiptoed closer to the back. The bus teetered back and forth, as the front end hung over the side of the bluff. The metal from the guardrail scratched the side of the bus with a blood curdling screech. Chloe screamed and sat huddled in her seat. Daniel tried to coax her to get up and move back to the door. Fear must have frozen her in place. I couldn't help myself. I took several pictures of children walking to the back, a picture of Mario and his little sister holding hands as they inched their way to the back, and a picture of Chloe's purple nails clenched onto the leather seat in front of her. I even clicked a picture through the front windshield of what awaited below, if anyone made the wrong move.

"Jett," Mike said, "put down the darned camera and get to moving."

"Yes, sir," I answered. Sammy grabbed my hand, and we moved to the aisle.

My heart was in my throat. I held my breath, as we all moved slowly to the back end of the bus, trying to balance the bus. We paused at bus six.

With every tip-toe towards the back, we felt the bus rock back and forth. I said a quick prayer, walking slowly behind Sammy.

EMILY

My mind raced all day, making plans for my science fair project. I barely remembered what I learned today in Algebra class or English. Throughout the day, I felt people staring at my hair, or lack thereof. Since I appeared to be fairly nonexistent, however, no one commented or questioned me about my hair cut, although I was hoping someone would. I was eager to share with someone my plans to devise a different molecular method of extracting DNA from hair.

No one asked me during lunch. Wyatt and Miranda, whom I supposed were some of my few friends, debated which *World of Warcraft* characters, Rexxar or Uther, they would be, if they had a choice. This heated debated went on for most of our meal. I finally interrupted completely off topic much to their dismay, asking them, "Has anyone wondered why I cut my hair?"

I could've sworn I heard crickets in the background when no one around me asked. As if I never existed, their eyes reverted back to their *World of Warcraft* cards and they continued in their heated discussion. Assuming further explanation would draw their attention, I spoke over them, explaining to them, "I cut my hair to use the debris in my science experiment. I knew it will be difficult to validate the experiment since I have to use my hair instead of someone unknown, but it was the only way to obtain recent hair shafts for this experiment."

Contrary to my expectations, no one responded with awe, "Why, Emily, whatever happened to your long, mousy hair?"

No one asked me, "Why, Emily, did you cut your hair off to collect materials for your next scientific experiment?"

No one even mentioned my favorite crime scene investigation show.

Despite the fact no one asked, I continued a detailed explanation of my experiment in partial whispers, waiting for my so-called friends to express interest. No one listened. Instead, my classmates continued their card game, a game lacking intellectual stimuli and its entire premise was absurdly unrealistic. Alone to meditate on my experiment, I left lunch to sit in the library to read more about hair follicle research. For the next three periods, the clock ticked along slowly. I watched it like a bomb would detonate at three o'clock.

Teacher after teacher lectured on subject-matter far below my intellectual understanding. Thus, while I plotted my future experiments, I sketched my next favorite thing—next to crime scene investigations—wolves. No one seemed to find significance in my research findings, but that didn't matter to me. Although I tried to speak to my teacher in layman's terms about independent and dependent variables at length, dumbing it down as much as I could, I wasn't even sure he understood. He listened to my extensive explanation with a glazed look on his face all too familiar to me; the unresponsive teacher nodded and grunted in response.

Since August I sat in his class and never learned one new concept. Sketching a wolf howling at the moon, this waste of time called class was an utter disappointment. This class was supposed to be the beginning of my advanced coursework. I looked forward to it for years. Here it was and utterly disappointed by the low expectations and lack of depth in the content. The teacher didn't even seem to notice half of the class ignored him. I delved far deeper than any other student in their class, and when I grew bored and read ahead, I was told not to read ahead. As I sat in these classrooms, reviewing information seemingly from third grade curriculum, of course, I grew more and more bored by the hour. This boredom morphed into anger and resentment. Wasting time, we sat like zombies. The only saving grace for me throughout these days was thinking—thinking about Dr. Z, planning experiments, and sketching wolves—sometimes all at the same time.

Then, I'd ride home on the school bus, and sit with my mother in the kitchen to tell her about my day's events. She listened to my ideas for research, while I told her all about every thought whirling in my head and crammed cookies in my mouth. School made me so hungry. In my previous lists, I failed to mentioned food as one of my other favorite interests. Next to crime scene investigations and wolves, food was my next favorite thing in the world. People, especially teachers and the other kids in my class, were last.

"Emily, dear," my mother began as I sat in the kitchen, "I received an electronic message today from your science teacher who expressed concern that you appeared to be very disengaged in his classroom. Even during laboratory experiments, you half-heartedly followed procedures."

"He called those lab experiments?" I asked. "Sticking thermometers in water, to me, is not even an experiment. A kindergartener could do that."

"Well, according to your teacher, you haven't been paying attention, and you draw dogs instead of listening to him," my mother said.

"Dogs?" I yelled, shooting cookie crumbs across the kitchen table. "What an idiot!"

"Emily?" my mother admonished. "You can't keep calling your teachers names."

"Well, he is an idiot," I finished with no remorse. "He teaches us nothing of significance, and mistakes very descriptive of sketches of wolves as dogs. He's an idiot! The man even teaches a zoology course, but he couldn't tell the difference between canine

"Never mind about your pictures," my mother interrupted. "You love science. Why aren't you putting your heart into that class? I e-mailed him back and said I would talk to you about your distractive nature."

"While you're at it, mother," I answered, "please tell him to teach us something interesting. Half of the class sleeps the whole time he talks. The most exciting part of the class is the experiment he assigned for the science fair."

No matter how many times I argued with my mother and tried to explain to my mother, whose IQ was 118, my teachers were imbeciles. How did she turn on me like this? My mom knew about teachers and how they cited textbook misinformation like false prophets and trained us all to be robots.

Finally, the school day was over, and my stomach gurgled with hunger for ding dongs and my science experiment. Sitting in my usual bus seat, I mentally scheduled my weekend. Dr. Z began at 7:30, but I planned to record it and watch it after I started my experimentation. There was no way I could focus on Dr. Z while a pile of hair awaited my attention. Last night when my mother discovered I cut my hair, she shrugged. The shrug was indefinite in approval or disapproval, despite the uneven bob I left in the middle of my neck.

My appearance never was a concern to me. As long as my clothes felt comfortable and fit, anything was fair game. Matching wasn't a factor in my wardrobe. My mother gave up on trying to doll me up years ago.

Even the unexpected haircut didn't surprise her, apparently, because she never asked why I didn't ask her to take me to a salon instead of cutting my own hair. Staring out the window, I saw my reflection again. My hair didn't look too bad. The snow was still coming down at an alarming rate, but we would be home soon. As I continued mentally preparing to begin my experiment when I got home, I watched a red car come up behind us.

Our bus moved slowly along the two-lane road because of the snow accumulation. The car appeared to be in a hurry, despite the inclement weather. I couldn't see the driver from my seat in the bus, but Mike, our driver, watched his rearview mirror, as the car moved closer and closer to the bus. Before anyone had a chance to give the car a second thought, the lady driving the car attempted to pass our bus. I watched vehemently to see if the driver accomplished the task of maneuvering the car around our bus in spite of a semi-diesel that appeared out of nowhere on the upcoming hill.

Just when I thought the red car planned to go for it, the driver must have panicked because she ran her car into the side of the bus right next to Mike's window. Mike tried to overcorrect after the car bumped us, but the road was covered in ice. When he turned the steering wheel, the bus slid left and right in a horizontal manner, until it crashed right through the guardrail on the road.

The weight of the bus caused the guardrail to split, which I calculated along with the trajectory of the bus gave us approximately four minutes before the guardrail broke completely and sent the bus down the cliff. The passengers' exact weight was an unknown, so an estimated twelve hundred plus the weight of an average bus equaled approximately twenty-five thousand pounds. With all of these facts and calculations combating for attention, it didn't take long for me to come to the following null hypothesis:

The bus, along with the passengers, was in trouble. BIG TROUBLE.

My forehead bounced off the seat in front of me. The last thing I remembered were the sounds of screaming...and some of the screams may have been mine.

NEOVA

Lava Red Hues or Ocean Blue Head—those were my two choices. After school, Say and I planned to stay over at my apartment and put new colorful streaks in our hair. That morning my mom had left me note and asked me to clean up the house before Say came over, so those were my plans for my Friday night. Weekends were the best! Two entire days to hang out, play with make-up, get on the computer, and, most importantly, not see the snobs we went to school with.

Chloe was especially getting on my nerves at school. Ever since she started dating Keagan, she was worse than ever. Every time we walked by her and her stupid group, they pretended to sneeze and whispered names at us.

Another time Chloe waited until I walked by her in class, and then she said as loudly as she could, "Oh, my, Neova, that is a beautiful blouse! Wherever did you get it? A yard sale?"

Her friends laughed, and I hated them all at the same time. I learned a long time ago that if you said anything back, they were relentless. It was just easier to ignore them as if they didn't exist, even when it felt like their words jabbed you like needles. Chloe definitely was showing off lately, even more than usual. Say said it was because she was trying to impress Keagan now that they were dating.

Keagan wasn't quite the hottest thing in the world to me. I never understood why all the girls were crazy about him. Keagan reminded me of a robot. He dressed like everyone else, spoke in the same monotone, meaningless banter, and smiled like his lips were glued to his teeth. It was weird to me. Besides the fact that I was always suspicious of any boy who looked like their hair had a pound of gel in it. Any boy who spent that much time getting ready in the morning was hiding something, or at least that was my opinion.

To me, Keagan looked like every other boy in school. At Jefferson Junior High, all of the boys who thought they were cool, or tried to be cool, dressed the same, smiled with the same fake pearly white grins, and acted like they were better than everyone else. If I had wanted to fold myself into a gelatin mold, I might have been interested, but I didn't plan to conform....and I didn't plan for him or any of the others to think I would ever be impressed with their blandness.

Walking out to the bus, I tiptoed along the sidewalk, careful not to slip. The sidewalk was covered with snow, but it seemed like ice was underneath. The snow was still falling. Jett beat me onto the bus. She was sitting in the front of the bus with the little kids, which had been her new seat since the transformation. As usual, I avoided eye contact. It wasn't very hard since she wouldn't look at me.

On the few occasions we accidentally looked at each other, her face was pained. It was too hard to see her like that, so I immediately looked away. Jett was only a shell of her former self now. It was partly my fault; in my mind, it was all my fault. Say planted the seed, but I sowed and cultivated the seed. In the end, I took full responsibility for the seed.

By the time Mr. Mike pulled away from the school the front windshield looked like a piece of notebook paper. If it didn't stop snowing, Say's foster mom wouldn't drive her over. Chloe was on our bus, which was rare.

Great, I thought to myself, *she's going to be running her mouth for the next twenty minutes all of the way home.*

Just as predicted, Chloe started flirting with the boys, as soon as she found a seat. I wanted to turn around to her, as she sat closer to the back and tell her to shut up, or I would recall her flirting to her boyfriend, Keagan. If I had done so, my miserable days at Jefferson Junior High would have escalated from annoying to unbearable.

As our bus moved slowly forward, halting to drop students off, everyone continued to pass the time until their weekend fun began. One by one, boys who attracted Chloe's attention dwindled, as they departed at their bus stops, until there was only Daniel. Daniel was the only boy close to our age left on the bus. Most of the other kids were from the elementary school. Daniel was older than us and way too cute to be in Chloe's league—or any girl in our grade's league for that matter. I stared out the window, watching it snow and listening to Chloe's pathetic attempts to gain Daniel's attention.

She tried to talk to him several times with no success. While Chloe asked about his weekend plans and the weather outside, Daniel answered in monotone, watching out of the window unimpressed. Only two seats in front of Chloe, I wanted so badly to turn around and laugh in her face.

It took all that was in me not to turn around and tell Chloe, "Ha! What about your beloved Keagan now? You're such a freakin' flirt. I hope Keagan dumps you on your perfect, skinny arse."

As I enjoyed my imaginary scolding, Mr. Mike slowed our bus down even more and was muttering to himself. Everyone, including Chloe and the other little kids, seemed oblivious to the weather outside our bus windows. Our bus moved along the road like a snail, leaving only a hint of white trail behind us. I tried so hard to hear what Mr. Mike muttered to himself and into the bus radio.

"I can't hear a darned thing," I heard him say before he slammed his cell phone back into the dashboard.

Mr. Mike's words didn't matter. I knew his tone was full of concern. Mr. Mike had been my bus driver since I was in kindergarten. Since then, in the last nine years, the only time I heard him yell at us or appear to be worried was when I was in fifth grade. Mr. Mike was driving us home, and I was coloring when he told someone to sit down.

His tone was much like today, and he told the boy, "It's getting to be nail-biter, if you know what I mean, so sit your little hind-end down now, so I can get you home safely."

School was nearly out for the summer, so we were all wilder than ever. Mr. Mike slowed our bus to a halt and told us calmly that we were under a tornado warning. When some of the youngest kids began to cry and flip out, Mr. Mike reassured them. At the time, I wasn't scared at all. After a few minutes of sitting on the side of the road and watching it rain, the tornado scare was over. Mike pulled the bus along the road to drop all of us off. I anticipated the same outcome with all of this snow, just as I figured all of the other kids did.

I was wrong. As I watched out the bus window, waiting for Mr. Mike to tell us the scare was over, I tried to distract myself by thinking about how I would look with different colors of hair. Just as I settled on two streaks of each color, my head hit the seat in front of me. Our bus started to slide about the same time a car hit us from behind.

Profanities flew out of my mouth as quickly as our bus was catapulted in circles before hitting a guardrail on a steep cliff. The bus stopped momentarily, and Mike yelled for all of us to move to the back. My head still hurt from hitting the seat in front of me, and I could have sworn I saw stars. Since I was already closer to the back than some of the little kids, I stood up, but I didn't move until they got up to walk our way. The bus leaned toward the back again, and we all waited for the level bus to settle. Just as Mr. Mike, who was already standing, walked two steps down the aisle, following the smallest kid toward those of us in the back of the bus, another car hit the side of our bus, sending us flying down this huge hill.

Some of the kids on the bus were sitting when we got hit, but some were standing in the process of moving towards the back, so kids were flying through the air like a snowball fight. I wasn't exactly sure what happened the entire time, because my eyes were squeezed shut most of the time and I ducked my head under my arms like Mike instructed us back when we took cover from the tornado in fifth grade. My arms didn't hear instructions from my brain, but they just moved in the protection mode. Somewhere in the process of it all, another little kid who just about made it to my seat flew into me, and I grabbed her to keep her from bouncing around anymore. The little girl threw her arms around me, and we held each other the rest of the way down the hill.

In times like these, you didn't care who you were hugging, no matter if she was a stranger, you all were in this together. The two of us clung together and pushed our weight against the seat in front of us. Throughout it all, kids cried and screamed, and, at one point, I recognized my own voice crying out.

We kept our heads ducked and refused to watch where our bus was headed. After what seemed like an hour, the bus finished its downhill slide with a THUMP!

At first, no one moved. The screams and yells stopped briefly for half a second while we waited to see if the bus was going to start rolling again. I peeked my head over the seat, and there were hardly any other heads to see. Everyone else either had the same idea or they must have been knocked out in the floor or dead, or so I thought.

The only person left in the front of the bus wards the front windshield of the bus was poor Mr. Mike. His body settled in the floorboard nearly falling down the exit stairs.

My mind took a minute for what I saw to register before I screamed, "No! Mr. Mike, are you okay?!"

I released my hug of the little girl gently dropping her into our seat and started down the aisle to the front. Our driver was the only person who appeared to be dead. *Dead. Dead. Dead.* The word repeatedly recycled through my brain, as the shock of his limp body came closer and closer. His eyes were closed, and blood dropped from his skull where he hit something when we rolled down the mountainside. The windshield or the steering wheel? I wasn't sure, but, nonetheless, I screamed. How was it possible? Mr. Mike was dead.

BILLY

Today was much better than dumb 'ole yesterday. Every day of the week oughta be like Friday. Friday's we got our free food and watch movies all day instead of readin'. I figured them teachers tired of learnin' us, so they liked to have Friday movie day as much as us, kids. We got our bags of free food first thing in the mornin'. I never understood why they called 'em Friday backpacks when they weren't even backpacks.

They weren't nothin' but plastic sacks stuffed plum full of food, but didn't matter none to me what they call 'em, 'cause they had good stuff in 'em. Peanut butter in a tub, fruit packs, nuts, and even cookies. Not everbody gets a Friday backpack, but even if we had any money, I'd wanna get a Friday backpack anyway 'cause they were so good.

This was all I was athinkin' about when I stepped foot on the bus to go home after school. I planned to eat part of the food as soon as I got home. I was gonna sneak out to my tree house, even though it was so cold I knew I'd sure to freeze to death. All of the food would last 'til Monday when we went back ta school. Sometimes my pops and Cheryl went out most of the weekend to bars and stuff, so that way I didn't haveta worry about what I ate.

When I got on the bus, I plopped down in my assigned seat, can't believe how much it was snowin' out the winder. Mr. Mike, our bus driver, musta forgot to warm up the bus, 'cause it was still purty darn cold on it. One boy who lived in a trailer nextta us, Mario, was sittin' with me and kept pokin' at me. I jabbed back at 'em with my pencil I was achewin' on.

We took turns doin' this for a while. The snow kept comin' down real good, and I was thinkin' I might oughta take the trailer park's trash bin lid and ride it down the big 'ole ditch. Mario liked to sled too. Spare'd come along, but her big butt didn't fit on the lid prolly. Boy, it was snowin' even harder now. When the bus stopped to drop off other kids, those kids got on up and ran off the bus to their houses. Them houses looked purty warm.

'Nother good thing 'bout Friday was my Dad got off work early and was already home when I got off the bus. I knew when I got home, he'd be sittin' in front of the TV with a Busch beer, askin' Cheryl, "Whatcha plannin' on feedin' us, woman?"

Cheryl talked at us much sweeter when Daddy was home. I guessed she knew he'd send her apackin' if she was too mean to us. I was thinkin' 'bout all of this when I noticed our bus was startin' to slide a bit on the road. Now snow was comin' down so much I couldn't even tell where the road was.

Mr. Mike slowed us down, and we creeped down the road slower than a turtle. The other kids got quieted down and they musta been a little nervous like me. Right when we got close to Dead Man's Curve, a big sharp bend in the road, I held my breath. Then just like that a car hit us in the back like a bumper car at the fair.

What the heck? My head hit Mario's shoulder, and we both got bumped up high in the air. Then we went slidin' down a big hill like a sled. I screamed fer mama the whole way down, even tho I knowed I hadn't seen 'er in a really long time. Funny to me she was the one I hollered fer, but that was who I hollered fer. I bounced over Mario, and my head hit the winder when we stopped. I looked 'round and everbody was ascreamin' and ahollerin'. My dirty fingers never let go of my food bag and my tored-up backpack the whole way down the hill. If I hadn't been so scared with it all, and, if my head wasn't throbbin' like crazy, I thought, this mighta been kinda fun.

MRS. POWELL

At 4:30 p.m. sharp, I forced myself out of my desk. I decided I should head home from school. I gathered up all of my papers to grade over the weekend. Years ago, I made a rule for myself. I would not grade any papers until Sunday afternoon. I didn't even realize it was snowing so hard outside until I made it upstairs to the main level of the school building and could see out the front glass doors.

I was accustomed to being tucked away without any windows in my classroom. If I had known it was snowing so badly, I would have left school earlier. I wondered if my husband made it home yet. The roads were probably pretty slick by now, and I didn't look forward to trying to drive home either. I pulled my coat on, and walked out to my car.

By the time I made it home, my nerves were shot. My eyes ached from reading all day at work and then staring through the white sheet of snow coming down in front of my windshield. My husband's truck wasn't in the driveway yet, but I figured he would be home before dark. In the meantime, I planned to sit in my recliner watching my soap operas recorded from earlier in the day. Soaps were a habit I couldn't break. No one knew it was my secret tool of escapism.

When I turned the television on, the five o'clock news was in the middle of a breaking story. The news reporter stood bundled in a bright pink coat and matching scarf, and her hair was perfect despite the inclement weather.

"Yeah right," I muttered to myself. "Your hair must have three bottles of hairspray on it. It hasn't moved an inch out in the snow."

Talking to myself was another habit I couldn't break. I was so focused on the reporter's hair I nearly missed seeing the building behind her. Where was she? Was she standing in front in the parking lot of Jefferson Junior High? It had to be. I turned up the volume with the remote to hear the big-haired reporter.

"News Channel 9 is still at the scene of Jefferson Junior High, where the school district's superintendent recently reported one of the district's school buses has not returned from its afternoon route," the reporter explained, staring concerned into the camera. Snow continued to pour down around the reporter.

The camera scanned to the school's parking lot where several people sat in cars, and the reporter continued, "As you can see, many parents are already growing concerned about where their sons and daughters may be. The school district's transportation office first learned of the missing bus when parents called concerned when their children did not arrive home at their usual time. The transportation director reported he was unable to contact the bus driver on his transmitter radio."

Hearing the reporter talk about the missing school bus hit me like a punch in my stomach. Immediately, I felt sick.

The reporter continued, "Currently, Police Chief Daniel Donover is back at the station, leading the investigation. Chief Donover told us over the phone a few minutes ago that police officers are driving the same route as the missing bus, trying to locate it. The police say they most likely will find the bus broken down along the side of the road."

The reporter took a deep breath, flipped her hair dramatically, stared down the camera with a stern face, and finished, "Earlier, Chief Donover told News Channel 9 although this storm was slowing down his officers, he was sure they would locate the bus and return the children to safety in the next couple hours. We will remain live at Jefferson Middle School to keep all of our viewers informed, as this story unfolds."

My mouth dropped open, and my eyes welled up. Lifting myself out of my recliner, I wasn't sure what to do. Should I go back to the school to help in some way? The police had to find the bus soon, I thought. Right? The reporter shared the main roadways in her report, and I paced around the living room, tracing the bus route in my mind.

I resisted the urge to get in my car and drive the roads myself to look for the bus. Half of the route was side gravel roads into the country where some of the children lived. With the snow still pouring down outside, the roads were still covered. Along the route, there also were several curves and steep cliffs that were pretty dangerous in these weather conditions.

I wouldn't let my mind go there. Looking out of my front windows, it was obvious I wouldn't make it very far in my car in this snow storm.

My little car slid all over the slick roads on my way home from school. I decided to wait one hour and to watch the news to see if they find the bus with a flat tire or overheated on the side of the road.

"I *will* remain calm and wait patiently. I will remain calm and wait patiently," I repeated to myself over and over, pacing a path in my thick shag carpet.

CHLOE

The morning of our wreck, I remembered getting got out of the car just as Jett stepped out of one of the buses next to the curb. Although I could've easily caught up with her to say hello, I knew walking with her would be social suicide. I paused and pretended to text someone on my new smart phone, even though it was so cold already. Shivering, I sent another text, hoping she would hurry up and get in the building. I never would've told my parents this, but I should have worn my thicker coat.

My new skinny jeans and sweater didn't look as good with my thick coat. Jett walked past me into school with her face down to the ground and a stocking cap covering her new "do." I probably should have felt sorry for her, but I didn't. When I heard she was spreading rumors about me, I really didn't feel bad for her. Even though she was supposed to be my best friend, Jett also lied to me about everything. She told me she lived right down the road from me in a subdivision, but she really lived in a trailer park. Her house looked like a broken down camper. Aluminum foil even covered one of the windows. We always hung out at my house, but I didn't think there was anything suspicious about it.

Jett even lied to me about where her mom worked. She said her mom was a writer, working on her latest novel, which was why we couldn't hang out at her house. The whole time Jett lied to me. She lived in a trailer park and her mom is a waitress. Jett should have known I wasn't shallow, and it wouldn't have mattered to me where she lived. Even though I avoided her in the morning, unfortunately, now I couldn't avoid her in the afternoon, since I had to ride the bus home. Both of my parents had afternoon meetings. Walking out to the bus, I had to move slowly since my boots' heels were sinking into the snow. Another fashion faux pas for me. Keagan walked along beside me, saying he wanted it to snow all weekend. When I glanced up and looked at his profile, my heart fluttered. After several years of crushing on Keagan, he was my boyfriend. Jett's loss was my gain. Keagan said if it snowed all weekend, we probably wouldn't have school on Monday. I nodded in agreement.

"School sucks anyway," I said, although I loved school, especially seeing my friends. What really sucked was being home alone all of the time with nothing but a computer to keep me company.

Keagan didn't seem to notice he did most of the talking. He didn't ask me about my day or what I thought about the snow. This was our usual routine. Keagan talked. I listened and pretended to be intrigued. If Keagan wasn't so cute and popular, I wouldn't even go out with him. His two favorite topics were motorcycles and himself. Did I really even like Keagan at all?

Or did I want him, because he was a challenge? Before, when he was Jett's boyfriend, Keagan was a trophy to obtain, but now I had him. Was I getting tired of him? No matter what, Jett didn't deserve such a boyfriend like Keagan. She lived where she lived. Her mom, Merl, or whatever weird name she called her, was a waitress at a piece of crap restaurant in town. I wouldn't even use the bathroom in that place. As Keagan and I arrived at my bus, he bent down and kissed my cheek. His mom was parked near the sidewalk, waiting to drive him home. He just finished telling me he planned to spend his entire weekend playing video games, but I hadn't heard much of what he said.

When I looked up at the bus, Jett watched from above through a window on the bus. She saw Keagan kiss me. Her face was pained, but it was becoming harder to see her through the snow. Jett looked away, and I felt shame and disappointment in myself. Walking down the bus aisle to find a seat, I chose a seat near the back as far away from Jett as I could get and spent most of the ride home talking to some of the cute boys on the bus.

When the only boy left to flirt with, Daniel, blew me off, I jammed in my earbuds and waited to get to home to an empty house. Loneliness covered me again, making me as cold as the single digit temperature outside. The heated bus caused our windows to steam up, and I traced the word Lonely on my window before realizing someone may have seen it. My hand wiped the letters away with one swipe, but it didn't make me feel any less lonely.

Just as I rested my head on the cold window, nearly falling asleep, something hit our bus. My head bounced and hit the window, and my backpack slid from onto the floor. The next thing I knew everyone left on the bus was screaming, and, at first, I thought I was dreaming. I jumped up to see what was going on out of the front window, but it was blocked by little kids bouncing up and down. Our bus was parked in a guardrail, and the driver yelled from the front for everyone to move to the back.

Was this like really happening? A couple little kids made their way to the back of the bus where the only kids left were Daniel and me. Chloe stood in the middle of the bus. I hadn't said a word to her the whole way.

Little kids surrounded me, pulling all of the weight to the back of the bus. Out of the side window, we saw what awaited us down the huge hill. There were trees and more trees. The bus steadied back onto the road, but then something hit us again from behind. The bus busted through the side railing. Mike's head hit his windshield as we hit trees and slid down through more trees and even some rocks. My teeth banged against each other with the impact, and now our bus driver's head was slumped over. No one was driving this bus!

LATER FRIDAY

JETT

My first thought when I came to was where was Sam? My skull felt like an elephant mamboed all over my head. When I opened my eyes, I looked around for my baby brother. He laid next to me slumped over. Blood dripped from his head. There was so much blood. I put my arms around him, trying so hard to say his name. Every time I tried to scream, nothing came out. I wasn't sure if I should move him, but I pulled his limp body out of the seat towards me. His long, light brown eyelashes remained settled in slumber.

"Sammy?" finally escaped from my mouth.

When Merl gave birth to Sammy and brought him home from the hospital, I pretended he was my baby doll. From the first time I laid eyes on the precious baby boy, I knew Sammy was mine. Half of the time, mom was too busy holding down two jobs or spending her days off, drinking with friends in the kitchen. I was no longer alone hiding in my bedroom, waiting for the music to fade into sunrise. I had Sammy and took care of him as if he were my own, changing his diapers, making bottles, and dressing him up. That was my favorite part. I loved dressing him up and telling him stories. Sammy believed every story I told him, even how one day we'd escape like Cinderella to a palace.

"Sammy," I cried my voice suddenly more audible. "Sammy, please. You can't leave me. Baby boy, please wake up."

Sammy's body was lifeless when I lifted him onto my lap. His blood smeared on my face, mixing with tears pouring from my eyes, but I couldn't let go of him. How long I sat frozen, hugging Sammy, I didn't know. It could have only been a minute or two, but I didn't plan to move until Sammy came back to me.

"Here, let me see him," a voice shook me from my daze.

Emily, the one weird girl from another seat in the front of the bus, made her way through the bus aisle. She looked down at the children, most of whom sat and cried. The panicked cries spread through the bus like a pandemic. Emily rode the bus every day and, in class, she constantly raised her hand and answered every time before she was called on. She was like a walking Internet search engine and always gave the class more information than they ever really wanted. Although she was weird, strangely, I felt comfort seeing her familiar face.

"Jett, let me have him," Emily said in a soft voice much different than the know-it-all voice she used in class.

Emily pried my fingers off Sammy's arms. I was reluctant to let go of him.

Emily whispered to me, "Calm down, Jett. He's still breathing."

For the first time, I saw past the blood covering Sammy's hair and noticed his little chest was moving up and down slowly. Emily was right. My little brother was breathing. Gently, Emily took Sammy from me and laid him across the seat next to me. Emily's voice transformed from likeable to her normal, know-it-all voice she used in class.

"I can't be too certain, but it appears to be a head injury, which explains the excessive blood," she stated quickly. "Without medical equipment, we can't be sure whether or not he suffered a contusion, but we will keep a close eye on him."

Emily assessed Sammy's condition, as if she were working with a medical team. moved closer to watch her work on my brother. My own body ached from being tossed around the bus after the long, rough ride down that hill, but I was too fixated on my little brother to worry about my own body. I didn't even notice the mayhem around me.

EMILY

After the fourth rotation, the bus finished with a final thud, coming to rest in a thicket of trees. My notebook and pencil skirted out of my hands across the middle aisle, and I grabbed the seat in front of me. My other things scattered about the bus, along with the other backpacks. Mr. Mike was sunken down into the floorboard. A wide laceration indicated a head injury. I tried to shake him, but he remained unresponsive. When the bus stopped, the loud noise made my ears ring. I held my hands over my ears, closed my eyes, and yelled.

"Enough!" I yelled. "Shut up!"

Surprised they actually listened to me, I stood up, seeing injured children who needed help. Before taking matters into my own hands, I reached for my phone to call 911. It may be a while before we made it home. Then it occurred to me—Dr. Z. Dr. Z started promptly at seven o'clock. My cell phone read 4:37 p.m. A little more than two hours before Dr. Z started.

All week I prepared for tonight's episode. I was prepared for one of the most intriguing autopsy investigations of all time. Panic overtook me. If I didn't make it off the bus by seven o'clock, I would never know the cause of death for the forty-three year old woman found in her bedroom with third-degree burns.

My mother would record the show for me to watch, if I wasn't home in time, unless she was out helping the police find us. I looked back at my phone. It was now 4:38 p.m. I tried to call my mother to tell her to stay home, abandon the search committee, and record Dr. Z. My phone wouldn't allow me to call out.

"Does anyone have a signal?" I yelled throughout the bus. It was much quieter now that I had provided medical care, but this was a far more important emergency. "Anyone?"

Everyone shook their heads no.

"I ain't got no phone," one little boy said.

"Mine's almost dead, but I tried and couldn't get out," one boy in the back said.

"My phone's out of minutes," Jett said, holding her phone up. "I tried to text, and it wouldn't go out."

How was it possible my phone reached a satellite to tell time, but I couldn't get a signal to make an outgoing phone call? Each passing minute was another minute closer to missing Dr. Z. I tried calling home three more times.

Luckily, the majority of the kids on our bus had already made it home. Counting myself, there were eleven remaining passengers on the bus. Around me, four elementary kids slumped in their seats and cried. Two of the kids cried, but they weren't injured. The third little kid had a bloody nose. He cried while he held his sleeve up to his nose. The boy must have smashed his nose on the seat in front of him. I moved up to the boy and showed him how to tilt his head to stop the bleeding.

The new voice I used was an impersonation of doctors on that television show about hospitals I never watched because it was very unrealistic. The plots were so predictable. By checking the little boy's heart rate, I noted if his heartbeat continued to excel, it would cause his nose to bleed. Last year, Dr. Z solved a murder mystery of an elderly man who was found in his recliner surrounded in his own blood. Come to find out, he bled to death when the old man suffered a nosebleed he couldn't stop.

Looking around at the children and the bus driver, laying in the front aisle, it appeared there were no fatalities. While some passengers were injured, surprisingly, we all survived the wreck without more serious injuries. As I moved down the middle aisle, looking at the children in the seats, I saw a girl hugging a little boy in a seat a couple rows back from me.

Her name was Jett, a classmate who recently appeared at school with a new hair-cut. When I first saw her in the cafeteria, I made the mistake of asking her for the remains of her hair. My hypothesis was the hair could be utilized as part of my materials necessary for my upcoming experiment.

As I saw her in the bus seat with the little boy, I knew from months of riding the school bus, the little boy was her brother. My previous observations indicated Jett was very protective of the little boy. I approached them and took him out of her hands, tending to his wounds. I used the same voice I used previously with children.

After taking care of a few other children and minor wounds, I looked up again to see Jett had moved and was standing at the front of the bus, hovering over our driver, Mike. Jet asked another girl, who I'd seen before on the bus and in class. She was friends with a few others who enjoyed tormenting me next to my locker. The girl wasn't the ring-leader in my bullying, per se; however, she was a member of this team. Therefore, I immediately felt disdain for her presence, even if we were in an emergency situation.

"Are you sure he isn't dead?" Jett asked another girl with dyed black hair and thick eyeliner.

"I'm not sure," the other girl said, moving her fingers up and down his arm, searching for a pulse. The dumb girl, of course, didn't know to find the radial artery in the wrist or the carotid artery in the neck. I wondered how a person made it to junior high without learning how to effectively take a person's pulse. Everyone knew you have to place your two fingers over the radial artery, which runs in between the bone and tendon. This imbecile rubbed her whole palm over our driver's brachial artery and median cubital vein.

"Move, and let me do it," I said anxiously, abandoning the fake doctor voice. "It appears he hit his head on the metal window pane or possibly the steering wheel. The frontal and temporal parts of the skull are already swelling. His pulse is slow, but at least there is one."

"Is he alive?" the girl with too many piercings asked.

"Yes, for now," I answered matter-of-factly. "He's obviously unconscious. Without a CT scan or MRI, I can't say for certain, but he probably suffered a diffuse axonal injury."

"What exactly does that mean?" Jett asked from the seat behind the driver. "Is he going to die?"

"There is no way to know right now," I said.

Even though I was focused on the bus driver, I also felt a strange sense of worry. I'd repeatedly watched surgeons on-line perform ventriculostomies on patients with traumatic brain injuries, but we needed the proper medical equipment, and it was too dangerous.

"Although I'd really like to perform a ventriculostomy to relieve the pressure on his brain, we probably should wait and monitor his condition for at least twenty minutes to see if he wakes up on his own," I continued.

"Ventrawhat?" one of the other little boys on the bus asked.

"I said ventriculostomy, which is a procedure during which you drill into the patient's skull and drain excess fluid," I explained.

"Ooh! Ya thinkin' about cuttin' into his head?" the boy exclaimed. "I ain't gonna be able to watch that. I'll puke all over everything."

Our bus driver laid flat in the floorboard next to his driver's seat. The front windshield was shattered, and the side window was broken too. I walked down the aisle three seats to front of the bus to examine Mike's injuries. I assured her and the others for the fifteenth time.

"Yes. I checked his pulse. It's faint, but he has a pulse. He has a large contusion on his left temple where his skull apparently struck the side window; it appears he's comatose, at this time. The word coma comes from the word *koma*, which means 'state of sleep.'"

"So, he's alive?" Jett interrupted, "Can't we wake him up?"

"There's nothing we can do for him at this time," I answered. "He may awaken soon on his own, but there's no way to know for sure. We'll have to keep someone by his side until the police come to find us."

"*If* they find us," Neova answered. She was on the verge of crying again. I also felt a pang of worry, but tears rarely came to my eyes.

Neova continued, "Considering the experience of our local police department, it will be a long shot, if they will find us."

It didn't appear my statements made the other bus passengers feel any better.

I continued to provide detailed background on the local police department, including officers' backgrounds, as well acknowledging there would be a search party gathering to find us, but probably not as soon as they should be.

"Police Chief Daniel Donover has served as chief for approximately three years after only two years as an officer, which means that he has a mere five years of law enforcement experience," I explained to them.

"How do you know all of this?" Jett asked me, after listening in disbelief. "Are you making this up?"

"No," I answered, nearly offended by her accusation. "I follow our police department's website and check records on all police investigations on a regular basis. As I was saying, Chief Donover is a fairly laid back officer, and most likely waited two hours before beginning a search for the missing bus, just in case anyone happened upon us and the bus broken down."

"Okay," Neova interrupted me this time. "That is just creepy. There is no way you can know this for sure."

"Of course, I don't know this for sure," I answered. "I am making a prediction based upon the police officers' past reactions to unexpected events. For example, last June, a resident reported a burglary in which all of her jewelry was stolen. The police decided to spend their time looking into the woman's children and their criminal records, instead of considering the possibility that this was an outside job."

"What does this have to do with anything?" Jett grunted. These people were very dense. I wished they could keep up.

"What I am trying to tell you is this is an example of how the department functions as an organization. They are slow to respond, because they automatically only consider the obvious," I told them, speaking slowly. "Chief Donover is more reactionary than proactive in emergency situations. In layman's terms, he probably just began the search party today, since no one reported finding us yesterday."

People often interrupted me, and it became frustrating when I was trying to tell them important information. Most of the time, people didn't understand me. Too bad for them, I thought, they missed the best part of my dialogue. I intended to tell them I thought I knew our location and that we needed to plan a way to make the trek back to the nearest gas station. Instead, I kept this information to myself until I had a chance to map the trip completely.

"Well, I am trying to stay positive and believe they will find us and soon," Jett said shivering.

"Oh, yeah, you are Miss Positivity, so that should be easy for you," Chloe retorted to Jett and turned to me.

"And there's no way you can predict how they will react to a busload full of kids stranded in the woods in the middle of winter," Chloe said to me.

"She's right about a lot of her information," the quiet dark-haired boy in the back of the bus muttered.

It was the first time I'd heard his voice all year. He just started riding at the beginning of this year, but he'd never said a word. He got on the bus at a subdivision right after me. His house was a middle-class home with a well-manicured lawn. I'd seen an unmarked police vehicle parked at his house several times.

The boy continued, "She's right. The chief is new to the police department, but he was in the Marines, and he knows what he's doing. I wouldn't give up faith just yet."

"How would you know anyway?" Neova asked.

We were all shocked with the boy's sudden interest in our conversation. We all turned to look at him surprised he could even talk. His blue eyes, hidden underneath dark hair, pierced through me.

"I know a lot more than she does," the quiet boy said in a deep voice. "I should know...Chief Donover is my dad."

NEOVA

I couldn't believe this boy was the police chief's son. He rode our bus all year, and this was the first time I heard him speak. His eyes were so beautiful that I lost my breath when he looked at me. Every morning and afternoon when he got on and off the bus, his hood was pulled up over his head, so I never seen his face in full view. He was definitely one of the hottest guys I'd ever seen. He wore faded blue jeans, a gray hoodie, and ear buds hanging around his neck. Apparently, he heard our entire conversation, but chose not to participate until we mentioned his dad.

Emily clearly stuck her foot in her mouth by slamming Daniel's father. Now that she had treated everyone's cuts and scrapes, Emily sat back in her original seat, stacking her notebooks neatly in her seat. When our bus first got stuck on the guardrail, I just knew we'd call for help and we'd be found. After speeding down the bluff, bouncing off of trees and thick snow banks, I started having my doubts. Luckily, the bus landed on its wheels, but several windows were shattered and crap was everywhere.

Most of us immediately took out our cell phones, if we had one, to see if we got a signal. My phone was out of minutes, and I really only used it to listen to music. So, I wasn't much help. The little kids were either too young or too poor to have phones. Jett tried Mike's radio and cell phone, and she said both were dead or broken. The snow was still coming down so heavily we knew we couldn't all get out and try to make it up the to the top of ridge before dark. In fact, the sunset was brilliant behind the translucent snow clouds. Once it turned dark, the temperature would drop, and we'd be hard to find down here.

"Should we turn the bus off to save the battery?" I asked the group. My mom had left her car on many times, so I'd learned what can happen if you leave it on. "We'll need lights when it gets dark, which will be pretty soon."

With all of the knobs and buttons, I was nervous to turn the bus off. If I pushed the wrong button, we could roll even farther down the embankment.

"Yeah, we should," Daniel said. He carefully tiptoed down the aisle to the front and leaned over Mike to turn the bus off. He stopped abruptly. "You know what. We should find a way to keep the heat in a smaller part of the bus. Three of the windows in the back are broken too."

"We could partition the back off?" Jett answered. "Up front I saw a roll of trash bags we could hang from the roof?"

"How are we going to hang them?" Daniel asked. He grabbed the trash bags out of the floor. They'd rolled onto the floor along with everything else Mike had on the dashboard, including bottled water, paper towels, a flashlight, Tums, and pencils. As Daniel picked everything up and put it back on the dashboard, Sammy pulled the secret weapon out of his sister's bag.

"Jett! You got your striped duct tape here," Sammy yelled.

"Thanks, Sammy," she said.

Jett took the tape and she and Daniel barricaded the front six seats by hanging trash bags from the roof. It took almost the entire roll of trash bags to duct tape up a plastic wall from top to bottom. They used pieces of the leftover bags to cover all broken windows.

"I'll go ahead and turn off the bus and then we need to find out what everybody has with them," Daniel said.

"I'm hungry!" one of the smallest kids said. Several others echoed her.

"We need to figure out what we're going to eat," I said. Now that we were settled in to wait for help, we needed to think about feeding everybody, or at least the little kids.

"But we'll get cold!" Chloe whined. "We're going to freeze without the heat. We're going to freeze, if they don't find us soon."

"We'll be found before we freeze to death," Jett answered, glaring at Chloe. The two used to be best friends. After Jett and I were best friends, of course.

It was pretty awkward being stuck with both Chloe and Jett in close quarters. Chloe was still crying. She'd thrown a bigger fit than the elementary kids. What a friggin' baby. I saw no use in feeling sorry for ourselves. Someone would find us before too long. There's no way a bus full of eleven kids just disappeared without the whole town searching for them. As much snow was pouring down, though, our tracks may have been covered. The snow was so deep that it would even hide the broken guard rail.

"Jett, did you say you saw the car that ran into us?" I asked, grasping for hope of a witness to report where we wrecked.

"Yeah, but I didn't get a good look," Jett answered. Although she spoke to me, her tone remained distant, and she never looked me in my eyes. "I think it was red."

Daniel turned the bus off, and the motor went silent. Everyone was quiet for the first time since the wreck. The silence was eerie. We listened intently. I knew we all were listening for the same sound—the sound of sirens telling us help was on the way. Instead, all we heard was an owl hooting, snow pounding the bus roof, and a coyote howling in the distance.

BILLY

I didn't care how mean and ugly 'ole Cheryl was. I just wanted to get on home. Everbody took my plastic food bag and shared it 'cuz it's all we gotta eat. The one girl who took charge, Jett, made us all dump out our bags of stuff and share it all. I wasn't really wantin' ta share or tell anyone 'bout my food. The other weird-actin' girl, Emily, who was like a docter or somethin', tole on me and said I was hidin' a whole bunch of food under my seat.

"I need those for this weekend at home," I tole 'em.

They grabbed at my goodies like crawdads, but I showed 'em. I kept one pack of peanut butter crackers and dry noodles behind my back in between the bus seat and my butt. Nobody wuz even smart 'nough to think 'ta look me over real good. I ain't gonna sit out here and starve to death. Mario saw me hide 'em, but he ain't gonna tell nobody. I don't even know if he speak no English anyway. Mario made me a little mad though' cuz he didn't get his Friday backpack of food like he was supposed ta. We woulda had double food then, Mario, I thought. His arm was still bugged him, so I didn't push at him too much.

"We may not make it home this weekend, stupid," another girl saidta me. She was all dolled up like we was goin' to a birthday party not stuck in snow on a wrecked bus. I even saw 'er put on lipstick alittle ago.

"Ya ain't got no idear when we gonna be home, so shut up 'bout it," I spouted back at 'er. "Since I's the one who gave all my foods I oughta get first choice of what I wanna eat ever time."

The Barbie-doll wanna-be tried to take first choice. I ain't got no patience for uppity girls bossin' me round, so I snagged the food bag real good 'an quick. Sammy's sister, Jett, calmed me down right good by lettin' me tell everbody what they got 'ta eat. All I kept thinkin' after sittin' in the cold all night was I'd rather be all-hugged up with Cheryl, then be stuck out here in the middle of nowhere starvin' and freezin' half to death.

SATURDAY

JETT

Why hasn't anyone come to look for us? The driver in the red car surely knew she hit us. Rose! That's who it was. At first, I knew the lady looked vaguely familiar the more I thought about it. I didn't get a good look at her face, since it all happened so quickly. With the time to do nothing but think, I tried to find her place in my memory. Even if she didn't find help, someone had to drive along and see the broken guardrail.

It was a long, cold night last night. The bus was so dark, and everyone seemed to be waiting patiently for help to arrive. After the long night on the bus, though, and the remaining silence outside, some of the kids began to panic. Most of the small kids were still asleep when I woke up. The night before we, the older kids, tried to comfort them, assuring them that our parents would find us any minute. As I told one little boy, we knew we'd be found before we fell asleep. I had a gut-feeling I was wrong.

Before resigning to sleep ourselves, Emily and I tried to climb out of the bus to assess the situation. We thought we could climb up the hill easily and wave down any cars driving by to help us. It took us nearly an hour to get the bus door open. The door was bent, and a tree limb held it shut.

After we finally got the door open and made it outside, we realized how far we had rolled down the hill. It was freezing and the snow was so thick it was difficult to breathe or see our hands in front of our faces. It was dark by then and it was so cold it felt like the temperature had dropped twenty degrees since we left school.

"We can't make it far out here," I said after less than one minute outside the bus.

Emily seemed more desperate to try to climb up the hill despite the weather conditions.

"If we start walking now, we can make it home by seven o'clock. I have to be there when Dr. Z begins," she mumbled to herself.

"Um..Emily, it's so cold my eyeballs feel frozen already," I answered through the thick scarf covering my face. "Even if we made it up the hill, there is no guarantee we'll find anyone on the road. With this snow, everyone's probably staying home to wait it out."

"I suppose we should wait it out inside instead," Emily finally muttered, clearly frustrated. "Given the amount of precipitation, dropping temperatures, and slope of this hill, it will take quite some time to get back to the road. The human body expires if its body temperature drops below seventy degrees, which is highly probable out here."

We pushed the bus door open and got back on the bus. I wished Mike was conscious to help us decide what to do next. He still laid in the floorboard in a silent sleep. Emily continued to check his vitals throughout the evening. She created a chart in her notebook and recorded the numbers each time she checked his pulse.

"He's still unresponsive, but his vitals are strong," Emily mumbled, writing the latest numbers in her notebook. "Mike should make it, if we get help soon. I think we should turn off the bus engine though, or we could run out of gas."

"We probably won't be out here long enough to run out of gas, so I think we should just keep running it," Neova said. "It's better than freezing to death."

"We all hope help will show up soon, but I think we should be prepared to stay warm throughout the night at least," I said. I'd seen how dark and quiet it was outside. Darkness surrounded the bus, proof no one was near enough to find us. Sammy looked terrified too at the thought of turning off the bus.

After a ten-minute lecture from Emily about the diesel fuel capacity of the bus and the how long it will sustain, we all finally agreed to turn the bus off and huddle together in the front of the bus. Luckily, today was pajama day for the elementary students, so they all had small blankets and stuffed animals in their backpacks. Most of the broken windows were towards the back of the bus too, so it only made sense we should only heat the front half of the bus. Emily had duct tape, so we taped all of the kids' blankets to the top of the bus. The other holes were a little trickier, but we found trash bags in the front of the bus, so we used several of them, pulled apart into big rectangles and taped them to the side walls.

The smaller kids sat watching attentively, but their faces told us how they really felt inside. They were terrified. Everybody settled in the front seven seats and cuddled to keep warm. The temperature outside had to be nearing below zero. Drifts of cold air escaped through the windows' cracks here and there.

We decided we'd turn the bus on for five minutes every hour or two to warm back up. We left the headlights on for thirty-minute intervals as well, so we didn't run the battery out. We all agreed the lights were worth the sacrifice, since we hoped a passing car above us on the highway might see the guardrail and peer down the hill. Unfortunately, we were down the hill too far to even see the deserted road so the chance of them seeing us was only because of the lights.

While rummaging through the glove compartment looking for trash bags, we also found a flashlight, a box of tissues, a soda, a bag of mixed nuts, and some plastic utensils from fast food restaurants. There also was a first aid kit, containing the usual contents like bandages, hydrocortisone, antibacterial soap, tape, and gauze. Emily already used most of it, though, after the wreck. Huddled with the others kept us warm most of the night, but right before it was time to turn the bus back on to warm up, the air was so cold we could see our breath. My teeth chattered and my feet felt like they were going to fall off. Sammy's little teeth chattered all night too.

The question of whether or not someone would find us worried me. We couldn't sit still, though, and just wait. As much as I complained about my home, my mom, and my life, I'd give anything to be with my mom. This hair, my life back home with my mom, and the hateful comments at school were all painful, but I knew I would have taken it all back in a heartbeat, if it meant getting off of this bus.

EMILY

It was so aggravating when people didn't plan ahead. Here we were stranded in the middle of God-knows-where, and these people tried to eat every edible thing they found in one meal. Fortunately, I was smart enough to convince them to ration out our supply in smaller portions in case we had to wait longer than we thought for help to arrive. If it weren't for me, these kids would have starved to death in two hours. Jett was the only one who instantly agreed with my recommendation. The others finally gave in when I asked them if they'd like to freeze to death or die of starvation.

Of course the smaller children cried, thinking I was speaking literally rather than figuratively, so I had to retract my statements. The older ones understood the dire need to ration our food portions. We agreed to divide all supplies to make them last, just in case we were here any longer. I insisted every passenger on the bus dump their backpacks and purses to account for any supplies. Next, I created a table to take an inventory of all food and other supplies we had on the bus in case we needed anything. It took a while, but I convinced everyone to trust me to keep inventory, so we knew what we had to make it until our parents found us.

To be honest, I secretly hoped someone would have had a device capable of picking up the television station to watch Dr. Z. If not that night, the episode would re-run again the next morning. Another reason was apparently I was the only realist on the bus who watched the on-going snow and realized it would be near to impossible to find our bus until it stopped snowing. With TV's, cell phones, or Internet, we had no idea what the weather forecast was, but I could tell it wasn't letting up anytime soon. I didn't exactly voice this opinion, however, because I knew the children would begin crying again, which would annoy me even more.

In order to keep accurate record of what we all had to utilize while waiting for emergency personnel, I explained to everyone I'd keep a list of supplies. Everyone nodded in agreement, although I'm certain the younger children had no idea what I was talking about, but appeared grateful we had a plan at least. Although we all hoped the date I used wasn't going to be necessary, I felt it was important to include just in case we were stranded for more than one day. Two charts detailed edible items and other supplies we had in our inventory, if needed.

Here was the table I created with edibles and supplies confiscated from passengers donated for the general supply collection:

BUS #11 SUPPLIES ROSTER—FOOD & DRINKS

Item	Passenger's Name	Quantity
Hard candy	Chloe	4 pieces
Apple	Chloe	1
Beanie Weenies	Billy (Friday Backpack =FBP)	2
Ramen Noodles	Billy (FBP)	4
Jar of Peanut Butter	Billy (FBP)	1
Package of Cheese Crackers	Billy (FBP)	6
Half turkey sandwich	Chloe	1/2
Bottled Water	Mr. Mike	2
Coca Cola	Mr. Mike	2 cans
Bottled Water	Jett	1
½ candy bar	Daniel	1/2
Beef Jerky	Daniel	2
Chocolate Pudding	Billy (FBP)	4
Can of Chicken Noodle Soup	Billy (FBP)	2
Cheese Puffs	Sammy	1 Bag

BUS #11 SUPPLIES ROSTER—OTHER MISCELLANEOUS MATERIALS

Item	Passenger's Name	Quantity
Duct Tape	Jett	2 rolls
Cell Phone w/ music (no signal)	Jett	1
Baby Wipes	Chloe	1 Package
Flashlight	Mr. Mike	1
First Aid Kit	Mr. Mike	1

After reviewing our inventory, I informed the older passengers, we had approximately three meals remaining to feed our total of eleven. This meal-count was calculated using the Calories of all items totaled divided by the required Calorie intake times number of people on the bus. It was a fairly simple calculation. The most difficult part was determining what the total Calorie intake should be for each person. Realistically, we all could survive eating hardly anything and only drinking water. However, we were not privy to when we would be discovered, so we needed to sustain an energy level sufficient enough to walk at least one mile, if we needed to.

In my calculations, I also considered the possibility we could be stranded for more than five days, which would mean we needed to spread out the Calorie intake as much as possible. I briefly described this process to some of the others, but I knew I lost them after defining a Calorie.

"When I say meal, I am obviously loosely referring to a meal as a cracker, piece of some sort of protein, and a piece of fruit," I explained to the others.

They appeared to be somewhat concerned. I still didn't think they had any idea of what we could be in for, based upon the continuing snowstorm. I chose not to say anything more specific about our status.

However, I provided them with an update on Mr. Mike, our driver's condition.

"Mr. Mike is still comatose," I said. "As of now, we can allow him to remain as he is. If time elapses too much, we will need to insert a feeding tube, so he receives the necessary water and nutrients."

"A feeding tube?" Jett asked. "How exactly would we do that?"

"I have an idea of how we could use a small tube from the bus' engine after it is sterilized, of course, but I will need help inserting it into his throat. I've never actually done it, but don't worry, I have seen it on TV."

"Are you kidding us?" Chloe asked. I was surprised she even understood what I was talking about.

"You seriously plan to shove a tube down our bus driver's throat, and you've never done it? What if he chokes?"

"Chloe, why do you have to be so pessimistic?" Neova answered before I could elaborate on my plan to use a feeding tube on our bus driver.

Chloe's questions didn't necessarily hurt my feelings. They only reassured me Chloe didn't have a whole lot going on upstairs, other than planning her next outfit.

Jett continued, following Neova's lead, "If you didn't notice Emily seems to know what she's doing, and I, for one, believe in her. We have to do something to help Mr. Mike. We have no other options, Chloe. What's our other alternative?"

"Whatever," Chloe said. "You guys do what you got to do. I don't want any part of shoving anything down Mr. Mike's throat though. If he like chokes, I don't want that on my conscience."

MRS. POWELL

By mid-day Saturday, there was still no word from anyone at the school or the police department. I had called at least ten times the night before and by ten o'clock a.m. Saturday, searching for new information.

Every time, the dispatcher gave me the same answer, "We understand you are concerned, Mrs. Powell, but we promise we'll call you as soon as we find them."

I knew I wasn't the only one calling the police station, but I couldn't fight the urge each time I picked up the phone and dialed the number. A path was worn through my living room carpet. When my pacing became too repetitive, I started making a figure eight, pacing through my living room, kitchen, bathroom, and bedroom, returning to the thick carpeted living room. I finished each circle through my house with a long look out the picture window facing the road.

No traffic. No headlights. Nothing left outside, but a steady stream of thick snow. The snow hadn't stopped for the entire two days, and the whiteness outside of my window made me nauseous. On the local news station, volunteers trekked through the countryside, searching for the missing bus. The reporter said there was still no sign of a wreck.

> It's as if the bus just disappeared. According to officials, the ongoing snowstorm apparently must have covered any tracks the school bus may have left. Now, on this Saturday morning, while most kids are watching cartoons, families of eleven children watch the television, praying for news of their sons and daughters' well-being.

You forgot one. My husband, I told the reporter, but she interrupted my verbal bashing.

> Driving the bus yesterday afternoon was veteran bus driver, Mike Powell, who has been with the school district for more than a decade. Mr. Powell was in pretty good health, the

> superintendent reported. Throughout the night and into this morning, crews have hiked through woods, searching for any evidence of Jefferson School District's bus may have left. Jefferson Public Schools has confirmed eleven children and the bus driver are missing at this time. The remaining students were dropped off at their homes prior to the bus' disappearance. None of the missing passengers have been identified at this time. The officials did say that once the snow subsides it will be easier to try to track them down.

Eleven children abandoned somewhere on a wrecked school bus. That was, if they survived the wreck. Where in the world could it have gone? The curvy roads between school and the last student's home left nearly twenty miles for officers to search. My heart ached to run out and find them.

Mike and I first met in elementary school. He was two years older than me, but since he was our only neighbor for three miles, we grew up as close as cousins. Mike rode his mountain bike down the gravel road to our little house. We went fishing in my grandfather's pond that settled next to the sawdust pile. When we grew tired of fishing, we rode our bikes up and down the sawdust pile, which continued to mushroom from grandpa's lumber mill.

Mike collected things—baseball cards, arrowheads, stamps, coins—even back then. Every year it seemed he had a new favorite thing to collect.

When he got into something, he went full steam ahead. He talked for hours while we fished. Mike had hobbies to share with me. He would tell me about the 1911 faded wheat penny he found at an auction with his dad, or how he was going to beg his dad to take him to the river again to look for arrowheads.

To this day, I listened to his stories without hesitation. I never told Mike how I overheard my parents at night, talking about Mike's parents in hushed whispers when they thought I was asleep. They debated about whether or not they should drop food off at the neighbors' house when Mike's father disappeared for a week at a time on a drunken binge.

As kids often do, though, we both grew up and drifted apart. In middle school, we found new interests. We never even entertained romantic notions, or at least I didn't. Mike admitted to me later he always knew I would be his wife, but I really didn't see him as a potential beau. It wasn't until years later when I was working at our town's local dollar store, and I saw him walk in the front door.

Mike wore blue jeans and a button-up shirt, but the face he usually wore was gone. He looked sad and lost, but I loved him just as I did when we were children. He'd just returned from Vietnam. I supposed I always knew he would become my husband. I'd waited too long for him to come home to let him slip away from me again. And, as they say, the rest is history.

As I awaited word on the missing bus, I waited for Mike to bus through the front door any time. In between staring out the window and pacing across our living room, I broke down regularly. I checked my phone repeatedly for missed calls. I tried to keep busy with mundane chores like reorganizing my cabinets and cleaning out closets.

If nothing else, I told myself, it saved our daughter from having to discard useless items when we died. Who needs nine coolers anyway? I went through our basement, steering clear of Mike's "man cave" area, which was really only a woodworking station and three metal cabinets of various collections. What I found was interesting.

At some point, Mike installed a fourth metal cabinet twice as big as the others, and how I didn't notice it before, I'm not sure. When I opened the cabinet, I found dozens of canned goods, bottled waters, batteries, and enough Aspirin to last a lifetime, along with numerous books: *Be Ready! What to do in an Emergency*, *Surviving the Wild*, *101 Things You Need in the End*, and my personal favorite, *Surviving a Zombie Apocalypse.* Mike's favorite television show of late was *Apocalypse Preppers*, a series I found entertaining and quite humorous. We watched an episode just last week, and I recalled how I had laughed when one prepper described her underground bunker.

I chuckled when the woman said, "We know we best be ready for anything. We know we are Americans…not Ameri-can'ts."

Apparently, Mike started a new collection with inspiration from our new favorite television show. It seemed he'd been working on this for a long time. Are we so disconnected I never saw him carry canned goods right through the kitchen and into this cabinet? I collapsed onto his old bar stool, and clutched onto his lucky penny sitting on his work desk. If they didn't find Mike, I wasn't sure how I'd live without him.

We didn't say, 'I love you' much, because it was understood. Neither of us were ever the sappy, cuddling type, but what I wouldn't give to wrap my arms around him right now, hug him, and declare my love for him. I couldn't sit here any longer dwelling on what I'd do without him.

My husband and those children were out there somewhere, and I had to help find them. If the professionals didn't find them by dark tonight, I decided, Mrs. Powell was joining the search party.

BILLY

That smart girl Emily done gone and poked Mr. Mike's throat, so he could eat. I watched the whole thing and helped her when she hollered for somethin.' Little Miss Barbie Doll sat coverin' her eyes with 'er hands and not helpin' a bit. I prayed again that the smart girl knew what she was adoin' when she poked his throat, but it seemed to help. She got the part outta the bus motor.

Watchin' her lift the hood was hilarimous. She was a hittin' snow off, gettin' fed up, and liftin' as hard as she could. Daniel hadta go help 'er. Emily came back on 'ta the bus with things kinda like straws. I didn't watch when she poked Mr. Mike, but I knew she got the straw good and clean before she went'ta pokin' on 'em.

She tole' me and the others she didn't wanna have'ta do it, but Mr. Mike didn't eat nothin' since our wreck. We all nodded when she tole us all about it, and we thought she oughta feed him, even though we didn't like the idear of her stickin' the pipe through his throat.

Daniel and Jett, that one girl, Sammy's big sister, who lives a few trailers down from me, done left. They went'ta find some help. So, we all follered what Emily tole' us. I kinda wondered why one of the other older girls, Chloe, didn't wanna help. She said to all of us that she wasn't e'en gonna watch in case Emily screwed it all up, and killed Mr. Mike.

Mario and his little sister don't know a whole lot of our same speakin' but they musta known what she was sayin' 'cause when she said the word 'kill' both of 'em got all sad and cried and stuff.

I tole' 'em that Emily ain't plannin' on killin' nobody, but tryin' to help, but they both cried like big 'ole babies. My dad sure is gonna be proud when he knows I saved all of these other kids and helped get Mr. Mike food. I talked 'em into cheerin' up and waitin' for the officers to come and fetch us. I ain't said a whole lot more to Mario 'cuz I don't think he knows what's goin' on anyways. We both been tryin' to keep busy with cards or racin' little cars I found in my backpack. I was a thinkin' 'bout how glad I would be when we got on home. That couch at home wasn't comin' too soon, that's fer sure.

CHLOE

My body ached from sleeping sitting up, and I would have given anything for a massage. From time to time, I felt myself float away from my body, out the bus window, and turn for one last look at the body of myself left behind. It was so weird. Sitting here with nothing to do was really freakin' with my head. If I had Internet on my phone or a movie or something, I would have been able to entertain myself days on end. Without any distractions, I wasn't sure how long I'd be able to wait. Patience was never one of my strong points.

In English, last semester we read several good books. Of course, in class I pretended not to care, but secretly at home, when my mom and dad were at work, as always, I read the novels, visualizing what it was like to be the character. We read one novel together about a boy stranded in the wilderness all by himself. It wasn't my favorite on our book list, but I remembered reading about Brian and how he struggled to survive. Brian was strong and survived in the end, but I didn't know if I could survive.....and remain sane.

Some of the boredom was passed by arguing with the little kids and watching Emily's endless exploits to help us survive. I knew I should do more to help, but my body hurt, and I just didn't have the energy. Other time was spent trying to talk to Daniel, which was probably the only excitement on the bus at all. He usually didn't pay much attention to me, but I had nothing else to do anyway. Usually, I went along with whatever Emily and Jett chose to do like organize supplies and blah blah blah. But I drew the line when Emily decided to put a tube in Mike's throat. I told her to leave him alone. Once our parents found us, they would call an ambulance to get Mike. He would go to the hospital and be fine. If she poked him in the wrong place, she could kill him.

Emily disagreed with me, and spent at least half an hour detailing the procedure. With everyone else on her side, I had no choice but to go the back of the bus in front of the trash bag wall and cover my eyes. I closed my eyes and played a song on my phone. When Neova tapped me on the shoulder to tell me it was done, I refused to look at Mr. Mike again. I couldn't look to see what they'd done. Emily reported the procedure was successful, but she said we would have to be careful to keep the incision from getting infected. Where in the heck did Emily learn how to do all of this stuff?

As annoying as Emily was, secretly, I admired her and everything she knew. If she weren't with us, we all would have eaten all of our food at once and then starved. Jett was being nice to me too, despite how I treated her at school. I mean we weren't like all BFF again, but she handed me food like she did everyone else and passed around the water bottle to me. She never brought up the names I called her. If I were her, I would've spit in her water.

I made sure not to let anyone know I secretly admired them. That's what I had done all my life. Pretended. Make-believe I was cool and couldn't stand people who I really liked. Pretended some more. Pretended I didn't want to cry for my mom and I wasn't going crazy inside my own head with all of the silence and boredom.

After settling back in my seat, I went back to staring out the window. What else was there to do?

SUNDAY

JETT

Just as Daniel and I agreed yesterday, we planned to embark on our journey to find help. I volunteered for several reasons. I was becoming too claustrophobic on that bus. I'd only been on an elevator once in my life, and that was all it took to teach me the fear of being closed in. Any more time spent in the confines of the bus walls would have resulted in a third degree panic attack. It was time to try to find help, and not wait for help to find us.

Daniel was awake having already packed our few parcels of allotted food portions, when I left my seat with Sammy to join him. The night before, like every other night at home, my little brother instructed me, "Hug my back." We fell asleep with my arms wrapped around his little torso. The smell of his hair was like incense in my nose, as always, and put me away to sleep.

We were still stranded in the middle of nowhere, and we couldn't just sit around waiting for something to happen. Out of the window, snow continued to fall heavily. I hoped we would awaken to a sunny sky without snow clouds, but that wasn't the case. I packed a small bag to carry, since I chose not to before we went to sleep. I held out in hopes we'd be found. Apparently, we needed to move on to Plan B.

Daniel and I ate a little. We were too nervous to eat too much, which was a good thing, since we were down to only a small pile of edibles. We packed a little food to take with us, but our wishful thinking led us to only pack enough for two small snacks at the most. Emily kept track of all our supplies and food in her notebook. All of us trusted her and let her tell us what we were allowed to eat for each meal. However, the term meal was an overstatement as to what we ate. A cracker and drink of juice didn't constitute a meal in my mind, but we were able to have some sort of nourishment, so we were all grateful. As far as food went, we all seemed to understand the importance of only eating our share, even though the little boy, Billy, appeared to have snacks in between.

I considered calling him on it, but he looked so pitiful in his dirty coat, and I knew his home life was far worse than mine and Sammy's, so I pretended not to notice when he snuck food from behind his back. The poor kid didn't even share with his older sister, Spare. I, on the other hand, acted like I was full after half of my "meal," so Sammy ate the rest. It took a lot of convincing, but he hadn't heard my stomach growling, so he believed me when I said I'd had enough to eat.

As we packed our small bags, Emily took charge. I hated leaving Sammy, but I had seen what a tight ship Emily ran, so I knew she'd keep an eye on him, while I was gone. I'd hoped to only be gone a few hours anyway, before finding help.

"Passengers," she began, much more formal than anyone else expected, "I propose we allow Jett and Daniel to consume additional calories prior to their trip."

"No," quickly I responded, "I haven't had much of an appetite, but Daniel might need it."

"No, I'm good," Daniel said. "I'll eat the same as everyone else."

Daniel had bags under his eyes, and I knew he was hungry. He was the biggest one on the bus, besides Mr. Mike. He hadn't eaten any more than the smallest kid on the bus.

"No, really, Daniel, don't be a hero," I said. "You really need to eat enough to give you strength. Who knows how far we'll have to walk?"

He looked around at the other children, and I could tell he took a second share with guilt. Looking right at Mario and Billy, Daniel said, "I'll eat a little more, but it's only because I'll walk really far for all of you."

"You're goin' to get us some help, so 'ya need to eat a bunch," Billy answered. As much as that kid liked to eat, this was the nicest thing he could have said. Sitting next to Billy, Mario only nodded. He hadn't said a word for the last three days. I wasn't even sure he could speak English.

"We'll be careful with the rations while you two are going for help," Emily said, counting food and supplies as usual and keeping inventory in her notebook. "We should have enough for a few more small meals for everyone until Monday morning. We then will be down to water only."

"Oh, we'll be discovered by then for sure," I interrupted, noticing the little kids, including Sammy, becoming frightened at her disclosure. "If they haven't found us by then, we can always hunt some rabbits or something. No big deal."

"How do you plan to hunt rabbit without the necessary weapons," Emily began. "You would need ….."

I interrupted her again with a harsher voice through clenched teeth, "I am certain, Emily, that me and Daniel will just take a few hours to hike up that hill and find that house on the hill and they'll call our parents."

"There was no house on the hill?" Emily added.

"Emily, there was a house on the hill, and we're going to knock on the door, find help, and come back to bring you all food and our parents," Daniel said. Both of our patience was wearing thin. Emily finally got the point.

"Oh, yes, that house," she said. It was obvious she wasn't very good at deception. "The house on the hill! Yeah, no worries. You two will be back in a jiffy."

This wasn't going to be an easy walk for help. We didn't know where we were going or what we'd come up against. We weren't even guaranteed to return alive. The camera would allow me to find joy in the trip, and I'd be leaving behind my last day, if something went wrong. It was a morbid thought, but real nonetheless. Sammy would know what I'd been doing on my last day, if we didn't make it back.

Before it got dark last night, we made a compass for the trip. Daniel said he used to be an Eagle Scout, and we'd need one to help us find our way. Luckily, he knew how to use his watch to make one. He dissembled his watch and told Sammy how to make one. It was so sweet how patiently he gave Sammy instructions.

"First, you hold the watch horizontally, as long as it's light outside. Then you force the hour hand to point towards the sun," he continued. We all were in awe at his secret knowledge. The little boys, Billy and

Mario, were especially interested. This was the first time Emily didn't even know how to do something.

"The next part can be tricky. You have to find the angle between the hour hand, which should be pointing at the sun, and the twelve o'clock mark on the watch," Daniel said. "The middle point directs you to the South, and the point directly across from it tells you where North is."

"Fascinating!" Emily responded and reached to grab the watch. Daniel held firm to the watch. "That's one thing I didn't already know how to do."

"I just got it right, so don't touch," he said. "I'll do it again tomorrow morning before we leave to make sure it was right."

The other kids settled back into their seats to play cards or to read before it grew dark. We all still persistently watched out the windows for help, but we knew it was a waiting game. If no help came for us by the morning, Daniel and I were venturing outside of the bus. Daniel and I sat together to finish up plans for the morning before trying to sleep. We planned to leave at sunrise and head back at sunset, if we hadn't reached help yet, so we wouldn't be stranded without shelter after dark.

Knowing we were going out together in the morning, created an unexplainable connection with Daniel. Of course, I still thought he was cute, but this went beyond how much I already felt my stomach jump when he looked at me with those green eyes that were a shade between leaves in spring and bamboo. In my mind, I clicked pictures over and over, cropping out only his eyes and long, dark eyelashes.

As we made plans for our journey in the morning, we were partners. Chloe watched with envy. She didn't want to leave the bus, but she would have liked to have an excuse to sit with Daniel. At least Chloe from Friday would have wanted to flirt with Daniel. The Chloe now, post-bus wreck, was an empty shell. She spent nearly all day, staring out the window bundled in her coat. Her only distraction was arguing with the little kids. Other than that, she was disturbingly quiet.

We had about an hour before dark, so we turned on the bus to run for the thirty minutes before sleeping.

This allowed the small area of the bus to warm back up before we slept. Turning on the bus meant hearing music, which was a delightful escape from the voices from other kids and the random silence that engulfed the bus of children from time to time, as we all fell into a cadence of thought.

The other kids finished their dinner, which consisted of crackers with peanut butter again and a piece of peach from a fruit cup, and enjoyed music before we turned the bus off again to save battery charge and diesel fuel.

"My dad says you need to know what direction you're headed to find out where you need to be," Daniel explained, as he took his watch apart.

"Are you and your daddy close?" I asked him.

"Yeah, I guess," he answered. "He works a lot. Police officers are always on call, so he has to leave all of the time. I'm used to it by now though."

"At least you have a dad," I responded. It came out so quickly. I regretted it immediately.

"You have a point," he said. "You don't have a dad?"

"Technically, I suppose I have one, but he's a little MIA," I answered. I wondered how Merl was coping with me and Sammy missing. "Sammy and I live with my mom. We call her Merl."

"It doesn't hurt her feelings that you call her Merl?" Daniel asked.

"You know I've never asked her," I admitted. "I love my mom and all, but she works a lot too. She's a waitress, and she works doubles all of the time."

A pause in our conversation followed. I'd been too hard on Merl. I knew she had to work for me and Sammy, but I often grew bitter when I was left to keep the house clean, to make dinner, and to watch Sammy all of the time.

"I miss my mom," I said, staring out the bus window, fighting back tears.

"I miss my mom and dad too," Daniel said. He went back to taking apart his watch. A lone tear fell onto the face of the watch.

"So, who wears a watch anymore anyway," I teased him, trying to change our somber mood.

"A habit, I guess," he said. "I put my watch on every day before I even put on my shoes."

After a group discussion about where we were and where help would be the closest, we'd decided which way we'd go. Daniel thought we should go in the direction of the longer route, because it wouldn't be as steep or dangerous as straight up from where we wrecked. We knew there wasn't a house for two miles from the point in the road we crashed through the guardrail. Daniel was afraid our energy would be expended before we even made it to the road. With the snow still coming down, there wouldn't be much traffic. From the last child dropped off to the last child not dropped off was a seven mile radius, we figured, so we knew emergency crews had a huge area to cover. That was, if they knew we wrecked.

Daniel said he feared the police would suspect a hijacking when they didn't see any bus trails.

"I know for sure my dad won't give up until we're found," Daniel said, as he put the watch back together. "Even if it's too late, my dad would never give up."

Words weren't enough to reassure Daniel I believed him. I didn't know his dad or his dad's determination, but I believed him, if he said it. I had no choice. Giving up wasn't in my vocabulary. Just as the thought crossed my mind, another voice reminded me just three days ago I'd planned to swallow more than a dozen pills. How was it possible three days changed me this much? If I wanted to give it all up then, now why didn't I just run out into the snow, lie down, and freeze to death?

All of the processed foods were doing a number to my stomach. The fact we were walking out into a snowy abyss didn't help either. My biggest fear in leaving was not being here for Sammy, next to freezing death. If I froze to death, that would still leave Sammy without me. Funny how only a few days ago, I was willing to throw my life away, and now I begged for another chance. I knew this trip was the last hope for me and Sammy, as well as all of the other kids.

Emily analyzed every aspect of us going for help. She was beginning to drive me crazy. Being stuck on a bus with a group of any kids would drive anybody crazy, I guessed. I slung my camera around my neck before putting on my coat and boots. Emily tried to stop me.

"Um, that's not such a good idea," she said. "You will need to keep your Calorie intake to the minimum to hike the tallest hills. A camera weighs approximately..."

I interrupted her again. I was getting more comfortable with interrupting Emily when she went on a tangent.

"I'm taking my camera," I said sternly.

"That's very unwise," she implored. "It may not seem heavy to you now, but after three miles, your biceps will tighten and possibly cause muscle cramps."

I didn't even answer her and continued to walk down the bus stairs. I wouldn't go without it. She continued to tell me I shouldn't take my camera. I'd never taken well to being bossed around, so even though she probably was right about the camera getting heavy, I now decided I definitely would take the camera. It went without saying, the camera wasn't only to document our trek for help.

The camera was as much part of me as Sammy or my new hair. My camera allowed me to view life through a lens. Then it was my choice whether or not to participate in reality. I'd become especially attached since my haircut. Even though it may be extra work or a burden, it was part of me, and I wasn't leaving it behind. Another reason for taking the camera crossed my mind momentarily, but I wasn't about to share this reason with the others.

Daniel and I left the bus and the other children and began our walk. He led. I followed. The first hour or so we moved slowly and arduously with only few words. We knew we needed to save our breath.

The first and only time I'd been to the beach was when I was ten. Merl's boyfriend at the time had an old RV and we drove twelve hours straight to Florida. We spent three days on the beach, and I didn't want to leave. Walking through the thick snow reminded me of walking through sand. It grew harder and harder to walk as we moved forward. The views of the ocean and warm sunsets also traveled with me, as I remembered how blissful the sun felt on my face. I pretended I was moving peacefully along the beach, as we trudged through the snow.

Daniel used his compass to direct us to the nearest house, or at least where we thought the house was. After some time of silence, Daniel stopped and said we needed to take a break. My stomach hurt, but I didn't want to be the one to ask to stop. We found an open area away from trees in a field where the sun beat down on us, so we would be seen in case another helicopter flew by. We laid down a trash bag on the ground to keep dry, sat down, and ate our small lunch. We each had half a piece of beef jerky and shared a fruit cup, before finishing with the staple of our diet—peanut butter.

"You know I have to ask you," Daniel started.

"I figured this was coming," I began. "I'd rather not talk about my hair though."

"My question had nothing to do with your hair," he said.

I had hurt his feelings. I could tell by his expression. He broke a piece of cracker in half and dipped it into the peanut butter. When we made it home—if we made it home—I never wanted to see a jar of peanut butter again.

"Sorry," I answered, tearing up. I was turning into a cry baby. "I shouldn't have jumped to conclusions."

"What I wanted to ask you was," he continued, "why are you so unhappy?"

The one million dollar question, and even I wasn't sure what the answer was.

"Um...I'll give you a few guesses," I started. "Is it a) everyone in the whole school calls me loser, ugly, or skunkhead, b) I have absolutely no friends except for a sixty- year-old cat lady who lives as a recluse, c) I haven't seen my dad in years and imagine our bus driver is my pretend dad, or d) my personal favorite, my hair looks like a chainsaw massacre took place on my head?"

My mood evolved from bitter to brazen. I had to laugh at myself. That all sounded pretty miserable and ridiculous.

Daniel laughed as he answered, "Well, I'm going to wager the rest of this jar of peanut butter on this guess. Could it be all of the above?"

"Ding. Ding. Ding," I chimed. "You are a winner. You keep the peanut butter."

We both laughed. It was the first time I'd laughed hard in a long time. For some reason, I laughed without thinking about the red stocking cap covering my head, a red, runny nose, and the possibility we might freeze to death.

"Your life totally sucks," Daniel answered, laughing again. "I thought I had it rough, but at least my best friend isn't a hermit."

"Now I feel ridiculous," I said, choking down more laughter. "So, why are you so unhappy?"

Daniel stopped laughing, looked down, and avoided eye contact. He answered, "Why do you think I'm unhappy?"

"Well, I noticed you on the bus before, and you're quiet and withdrawn," I began.

"Hm? You noticed me?" he asked flirtatiously.

"Yes, I noticed you," I said shyly. "I happened to see you get on the bus sometimes, and you didn't talk to anybody. You listened to music and just stared out the window all of the way home."

"Don't most people look out the window?" he teased. "So, if you look out the window, you need counseling?"

We had brought a lighter with us, and Daniel lit the paper wrappers with the lighter. We took turns holding our hands over the small fire.

"You know what I meant," I laughed. "I could tell there was a sadness with you."

"I wouldn't say I'm sad," Daniel answered. He held the small fire in front of me to warm my face. "I try not to waste my time getting to know people or making friends."

"Why?" I asked.

"We moved here last summer. This is our fourth town since I started kindergarten," Daniel said. "My dad's moved to get training and experience in different places. He says we're planning on staying here, but he's said that before."

"Merl moves us every year or so," I said, knowing exactly what he felt. "She gets tired of working at the same place, or we get behind on our bills. It's embarrassing. After my hair incident, I told her I wanted to move this summer."

"I thought you didn't want to talk about your hair?" Daniel said. My eyes watered from the cold. Daniel used his gloved hand to wipe the tear from my face. We were sharing the trash bag, so we were close enough

I could feel his breath on my cheek. I was glad it was cold, so I could blame my shaking hand on the weather. Daniel put his arm around me.

"That's warm," I said nervously. Please don't kiss me, I repeated in my head. After three days on a bus, I doubted the mouthwash was completely effective.

"You're warm too," Daniel agreed. "I really don't want to put my arm around you, but our body heat will keep us warm. I'm only hugging you for survival."

"Sure, you are," I answered. "I'm not complaining though. It's so cold out here."

"It doesn't hurt that you're pretty," he said, looking away at the endless view of snowy acres.

"You think I'm pretty? Even with my hair?" I asked sheepishly.

"Actually, you're not just pretty. You're beautiful….and especially because of your hair," he answered, turning his face back at me.

Our eyes met, and I felt silly for starting to fall for Daniel, when we didn't know what our futures held.

"One day I'll tell you the whole story," I started, but it was still too embarrassing. "We better get moving. Hopefully, we'll find somebody or something before dark."

"You're right," he said, beginning to put everything back into his backpack. He shook out the trash bag and rolled it into a small cylinder shape.

"You're cute," I stuttered through chattering teeth. "And you're good at folding trash bags."

"Well, that's a first," he said. "Let's get moving, so we can warm up a little."

We reconvened our march through the field and moved into another patch of trees. Since we didn't try to go straight up the mountain side, we were forced to make an arch to reach a point farther down the road, so we would be able to climb up the side. If it wasn't so cold, it would have been a pretty walk. The snow dangled from pine trees, and fat rabbits bounced across our path. The rabbits made me think about Sammy. We had to find help. I couldn't imagine Sammy having to spend any longer on that bus.

As the sun set, the orange and purple sky was picture perfect. I snapped several pictures. No one could possibly freeze to death underneath a sky that beautiful. Or at least that's what I told myself.

Daniel and I continued for two more hours. That's when the sky started to shoot sleet down on us. With nothing in sight to protect us, we were forced to hover underneath our backpacks and march with head down. Daniel said exactly what I was thinking.

"We're going to have to turn around, Jett," he yelled, so I could hear him over the falling ice and howling wind. "At least then we know where we're going."

"You're probably right," I answered.

As much as I hated the thought of going back to tell Sammy we didn't find help, I knew we would be back on the warm bus by morning.

"I'm sorry," Daniel added, as he turned around.

He threw his arm around my shoulders to block the wind, and we walked several more miles as one. Half of the time, he dragged me, as I grew so tired I couldn't barely keep my eyes open.

We continued when I thought there was nothing left within me.

"Keep it up, Jett," he repeated time after time. "You're doing good."

I'd lost the energy to even respond. Approaching the bus, I realized why no one had seen the bus. We hadn't even thought about it. Snow covered the entire bus, so it blended right into the mountain terrain. The lights and engine were off. Emily must have used her alarm clock to wake up and turn it off to conserve gas and battery. When we left the bus, I never thought I'd be glad to see it again.

"We made it," Daniel grunted. He pulled me up onto the stairs to board the bus.

"We made it," I repeated, although it was barely audible.

EMILY

While Daniel and Jett went out looking for help, I repeated my routine of handing out our meals and taking care of Mr. Mike. We also reviewed the last bag of food we had left. If Daniel and Jett didn't find help while they were gone today, we would be out of food tomorrow morning. I also spent some time taking of Mr. Mike. With the help of Neova, we rolled Mr. Mike over onto his other side to prevent bed sores. We had moved him several times throughout the past few days. After moving him, we wiped him down with some of the wipes. Neova followed her usual routine of speaking to Mr. Mike.

"You know he can't hear you," I reminded her again.

"You never know," she answered. We already had this discussion once. "I told you yesterday I watched a show about this woman who was in coma for ten years! When she woke up, she told her family she heard everything they said while she was asleep."

"Yes, you told me," I said, carefully covering Mr. Mike again, so we would stay warm. We continued to keep him hydrated, but I was worried about his status.

"Mr. Mike," Neova said in high pitched, happy voice, "we just wanted to make sure you had a little something to drink and you were warm."

Every time Neova spoke to Mr. Mike, she paused as if she expected a response. Jett spent a lot of time talking to him also, before she left.

"Well, I do recall reading a medical article that recommended speaking to a comatose patient for verbal stimuli," Emily said. "I am concerned he hasn't responded to any stimuli."

Neova moved closer to Mr. Mike and continued, "We are still out here in the middle of nowhere. Daniel and Jett went to try to get help. They're going to bring an ambulance to pick you up, Mr. Mike. Okay?"

"Can you hear me?" she continued.

Neova paused. I stood up and moved all of our supplies back into the seat behind Mr. Mike.

"Emily," Neova screamed. She scared me, and I dropped half of the items in my hands. "He moved! He moved!"

"What? Mike moved?" I asked, turning back around. All of the kids jumped up and moved forward to the front.

"Step back, children," I cautioned, blocking the front where Mr. Mike laid. I kneeled beside him. I didn't see any movement.

"I promise he moved," Neova repeated. "I was talking to him, and his eyelids fluttered. He didn't open his eyes, but I swear his eyelids almost opened."

We all stared at him, expecting Mr. Mike to stand up any minute. He didn't move again. After nearly ten minutes, we decided to leave him and returned to our regular activities of staring out the windows or playing Tic-Tac-Toe.

"I swear he moved," Neova said in a hushed voice.

"That is very possible," I answered. "And it's a good sign if he's moving, even if it is a minor movement. Comatose patients don't emerge suddenly."

NEOVA

I'm sure the others didn't understand why I continued to talk to Mr. Mike when he was obviously out of it, but I just knew that he could hear me. Even if he couldn't hear me I would want someone to try to communicate with me if I were in his position. Besides it helped me cope with what was happening to us in my own way. I decided to update Mr. Mike and explained to him that Jett and Daniel had went out to try to find us help when he faintly moved.

I couldn't believe it so I screamed at the others, "Emily, Mr. Mike moved!"

She darted towards us and the others followed.

"Mr. Mike, if you can hear me try to move again." Emily adjusted him into another position as she did often to keep his circulation flowing properly, as she explained to us everytime she did it. He didn't respond or move again.

"I promise he moved. I wouldn't make something like that up."

I tried to convince them to believe me, but I understood it would be hard for me to believe too if I hadn't really seen it. After a few moments everyone went about their business and Emily clarified to me that it really wasn't unusual for slight movements of comatose patients, and that it was a good sign for him to be making movements even if it was only a small amount of movement. I knew what I had seen and decided to hang out a little longer with Mr. Mike just in case. I just knew he could hear what I was saying.

BILLY

Jett and Daniel was brave. They done gone and left to go find somebody to come and pick us on up already. We all been gettin' so tired of bein' on this 'ole bus. The smart girl Emily say we ain't gonna have much food after tomorrow mornin.' I'm still burnin' over them done takin' all my food from my backpack 'cause when I get on home I ain't gonna have nothin' to hide in my treehouse. I ain't even really sure we gonna be gettin' home, so I shouldn't be countin' them chickens before they done hatched.

Ever time I get real scared, though, I've been bowin' my head to pray like the ole man at church taught me. Ever Sunday mornin' the old man picked all of us in a big van and took us on down to Sunday schoolin'. They been tellin' us if we need something purty bad and don't know what to do, we can just call up the good, 'ole Lordy in Heaven, and he'd be right there. In church, I ne'er really listened much or e'en prayed. I's too busy with my eyes open, and ain't nobody tole me this, but I don't think the good Lordy hears nothin' if your eyes been done open when you're all sittin' around prayin'.

Right before Jett and Daniel took off in the snowstorm, I tole everbody we oughta be prayin' around 'em. One time at Sunday schoolin' a missionmary done said he gonna go off to Mexico, or someplace I didn't know, to tell the chil'ren about Jesus. Before that missionmary left, we all stood in a circle in the front and prayed all about him. This there is where I got my idear. So when I tole' everbody we needed to stand around Jett and Daniel and say a long, drawn out prayer, they kinda agreed.

Spare just hadta get on up and tell everbody on the bus, "I was copyin' the missionmary and the preacher by askin' for prayer."

Nobody really cared that I was a copycat, I guess, though,'cause they joined on in with the prayin'. Everbody got in a circle and bowed their heads while I started prayin' in a voice just like the preacher. I was even araisin' my voice in just the right places. I done prayed, "Dear, Lordy God above, we are gathered here to join with these missionmaries, who are gonna go on outta our bus to find us help. We are a'prayin' for a hedge of protection to be all around 'em and angels too."

I hadta take a break and stop here, though, 'cause I caught Mario lookin' around while we was aprayin'.

"You ain't got much idear 'bout what I'm sayin', but it's a rule everbody gotta close them eyes when we aprayin' or the Lordy Jesus ain't gotta listen," I scolded Mario. "So, get them darn eyes closed before I gonna go close 'em fer ya."

Mario looked at me like he done swallered a lemon. I still don't think he aknew what in the heck I was asayin', but he did close them eyes.

"As we were asayin', Lordy Jesus, we thank you for your promisions and all that," I continued. "We are askin' with big hearts fer somebody to see our bus."

When I was done, I done knowed the Holy Spirit was a movin' 'cause I got little goosebumps up and down my dirty arms.

Daniel and Jett took right out after that and I was aprayin' still in my head.

MRS. POWELL

It could happen any day. ZOMBIE ATTACKS. One never knows when the Zombie Apocalypse will occur. With the recent influx of zombie television shows, movies, and references in popular culture, there must be more to this phenomenon. Experts report it could be any day. Do you want to be one of the few not prepared just in case zombies do attack the human race? The number one rule to avoid the catastrophe is to run when you see a zombie. The number two rule is to not get bitten.

I re-read a chapter in one of Mike's books, *Zapping Your Fear of Zombies*. Who wrote this book? One of my students could have written a better book. Did the author Kit O'Neal really believe people in their right mind would NOT run when they saw a zombie coming towards them? Did the author think some people might try to stop the zombie and console the blood thirsty killer?

Mike must have chosen this book for comic relief, or at least I hoped he did. Well, one thing I learned from reading part of the book I needed to take a rope. There was a whole chapter on rope and the many uses for it. I decided I also needed a flashlight or lantern, water, and, of course, my cell phone to call for help, if I found the bus. True to my word, I planned to go out and do my own search and rescue.

After watching the news all night, it was obvious the police focused only on a five-mile radius, using the home of the last student Mike dropped off as its central location. Hour after hour, I shouted louder at the television, "What are you thinking? Move on! You haven't found them, so look somewhere else, you idiots!"

Yesterday, waiting to hear news, I'd been dumb enough to log into social media. People in our area were speculating about Mike's missing bus. Many believed the bus had went over the Gascan Bridge and would turn up at the end of the bay several weeks from now. Some thought the bus slid on ice and went pummeling to the bottom of the mountain. We knew, though, that if that was the case there would be no survivors. I couldn't bare to even allow my mind to go there right now.

Several teenagers started a whole story about aliens abducting the bus and all of its passengers. How could anyone think it was appropriate to joke around about this? I just kept praying for Mike and those children. Mike couldn't die. We joked he had nine lives, since he'd escaped death several times in Vietnam and since.

I knew I couldn't wait around any longer to hear what the police had to say. Without a doubt, Mike would be out there in a heartbeat looking for me. I loaded my bag into my car, prepared to drive Mike's route. Back and forth from the school to the last drop-off. I drove back and forth twice, and then continued past the last drop off, since we really didn't know how far they made it.

The third time passing by Big Bend Curve I noticed something out of character. The guardrail was busted in half, which was only visible because part of the snow had melted off one side. I pulled over to check it out, even though it wasn't the safest place to pull over. I knew I couldn't not check it out.

The guardrail was, indeed, torn in two. The right side was curled out into a pile of snow. Where one would expect to see tracks, if this was where the bus wrecked, there was nothing but more and more piles of snow all of the way down the mountain. At the bottom of the cliff, there were only trees. No bus. I felt something there though. I went back to my car and took out a broom. I couldn't find a shovel when I packed my car, so I grabbed my broom just in case I needed it.

I returned to the broken guardrail and swept the mounds of snow off. Even though the snow looked like light cumulus clouds, it was much heavier than expected. I swept as much as I could from both sides, taking breaks to stop and make sure no one was coming down the highway. Only one truck passed me. The driver slowed down and asked if I needed any help, and I shook my head no. People would have thought I was crazy, if they knew what I was doing.

Once the snow was wiped away, there it was. I didn't really expect to see anything. It was like buying a lottery ticket just for something to pass the time to find you'd won. The front of the guardrail was stained with a golden yellow hue, matching a school bus. The more convincing evidence dangled below. Once the snow was removed, a headlight and a metal bezel hung from the rail, looped by the electrical wires.

Immediately, I knew I had to call the police. I ran back to my car to find my cell phone didn't get a signal on the mountaintop.

"We can put a man on the moon, but we can't get a signal everywhere in the world?!" I screamed at the mountainside.

All day I drove these roads for any sign of life, and this was all I found— a headlight. It was getting dark, so I knew it was time to go home anyway. As I shouted from the mountaintop, no one answered, but myself. I yelled two more times, just to hear someone respond, even if it was my own echo.

"Mike! Where are you?!" I yelled. For some reason, the reflected question comforted me. "I need you!"

• • •

Back home, our house was as quiet and lonely as ever. The whole drive back home, I'd imagined Mike's bus going over the side of the hill. Although I didn't see the bus, it could have been at the bottom covered with two days of blizzard snow. If it were covered, that would mean Mike and the children were inside the bus. My mind refused to visualize what that looked like. I picked up the phone in the living room to call and clicked on the television out of habit.

As I dialed the numbers, I saw the Channel 9 news reporter was at it again, telling all of us, viewers, how police were still looking for the bus. I just about clicked the television back off, so I wouldn't have to stare at her perfect, annoying face another second, but the reporter approached a woman with her microphone.

At the bottom of the screen, Channel 9 shouted with a banner, "*Late Breaking News.*"

"Please, God," I prayed repeatedly. "Please, God. Say they've found them!"

The reporter began:

> We are here with Channel 9 News with recent developments in the case of the missing bus. Police have not confirmed this yet, but we are at Todd's Trailer Garden in rural Jefferson County with resident Gwen Childers. Mrs. Childers, can you tell us what you've seen today?

The older woman stood erectly with an immaculate beehive saluting on the top of her head. Even though she obviously was not used to being on television, she was very articulate...and even beautiful in her own way. I recognized her from one of Jett's journal entries. Jett's descriptions of her home and of her closest friend, Gwen, were spot on. Gwen began to tell her story to the reporter:

> I like to pride myself on being the watchdog of our little community here. I could live anywhere in the world, but I choose here, for the children. Ever since Friday afternoon, I've been sick. Every night I watch those babies get off the bus and go on into their houses. None of them have much, but they're all so precious. When the bus didn't return on schedule, I watched out the window the whole night, waiting for them babies."

The reporter interrupted and asked Gwen,

> So, Mrs. Childers, what did you see?

The reporter grew impatient with the witness, which irritated me even more. It was obvious how worried the lady was. As the reporter and Gwen discussed the issue, several people mulled around in the background, wearing thick coats and none of them resembled upstanding citizens.

Gwen began again, stroking a fat, white cat,

> As I watched for the bus, I saw others pull in and out all evening. Some people just don't have enough sense to stay

home when it's snowing like this. People shouldn't be going out on them roads for no reason. But, anyways, I'd seen one of my neighbors pull into her driveway earlier at around three forty-five, which was a little early for her. How shall I put this? Rose has a routine and usually doesn't get home until almost dark or even later.

The reporter interrupted again,

Mrs. Childers, please try not to use names, like we discussed.

Gwen continued,

Oh, yes, sorry about that, honey. So, when Ro..., I mean this neighbor came home early. I told Princess, my cat, my neighbor must've hit the bottle a bit too early. When the neighbor got out of her car, she stumbled to walk on the ice and snow, but she stopped to look at the front of her car. At first, I figured she was doing a little up-chucking, but she rubbed the front of her car and went on in. I didn't think another thing about it until she returned outside a few more times and was spray painting the front of her car. Now, I see some bizarre things living here, but that was the strangest thing to see....a woman spray painting in the middle of a blizzard.

"So, you're telling us, Mrs. Childers, that you could see what the lady was doing?" the reporter asked in disbelief.

Gwen answered, pointing with long pink nails back at her trailer. The camera scanned over to her house. She explained,

You'd be amazed with all I can see from my little table in there. I don't like to tell people this, but I've got a pair of binoculars I keep just in case it's hard to see something. You see, honey, I'm getting older, and I can't see like I used to.

"What did you see with your binoculars?" the reporter asked, holding off a smile.

I looked real good and close at the neighbor and she was painting over a big dent in her front fender. The whole side of her car was dented too, and there were different spots with yellow paint on her red car. I just couldn't figure out how the drunk thought she was covering dents with paint. But then it clicked later on, when I was watching the news and worrying about the kids. Ro...I mean, my neighbor, hit that bus!

I kept watching out the window to see if the police came over to get her and watching the news to see the bus hadn't been found. I'd had enough and just called the phone number you had on the screen and told them what I saw.

The reporter asked another question, even though she already knew the answer,

"And then what happened?

The police asked me to come down to the station to file a report, and I told them I hadn't been driving my car in years, so they came to me. I just let one come in, and the officer came in to take my statement. The whole time the police car was outside, I saw the neighbor peeking out her window to see what they were doing here. I figured the neighbor hoped I'd just fell over with a stroke or something.

After I told them everything, they went over to the neighbor's house, looked at her car, and knocked on her door. I don't know what happened after that.

Thankfully, the reporter informed us of the rest of the story:

> Following Mrs. Childer's sharp wit and quick thinking, the Jefferson County Police Department spoke with the neighbor, and she admitted to playing a role in a hit and run. We expect police to hold a press conference at any time, in which they will release the woman's name and other information they have gained. The only updated news the police have given us so far is that the alleged driver involved in the hit and run told police she doesn't remember where she hit the bus.

I finished punching the number on my phone and told the dispatcher I had an idea where the accident occurred.

MONDAY

JETT

I knew we'd find a good use for these stale cheese puffs. We never would've found our way back to the bus without them. Everyone was so happy to see us finally return to the bus. But they wore fake smiles when we returned on the bus without help and all alone.

"How far did you make it?" Emily asked, marking on a map she had drawn in her notebook.

"We're not really sure how far," Daniel answered. "When it started to get dark, it started to sleet. It was coming down too hard to keep moving. We walked all day, but the snow was so thick, it took forever."

"My legs are like Jell-O," I added. I hoped they knew we tried our best.

"If we would've kept walking, we didn't know how much farther and were afraid we'd freeze to death," Daniel said. "We'll try again tomorrow, if help hasn't come. If the sun comes out, the snow should melt off some."

The little ones didn't seem to think this was their last chance, because they started crying with the news. The questions flew at us.

"Did you see anyone?"

"Why'd ya come back already?"

"How far away was that house we saw on the way here?"

The littlest girl broke my heart. She looked up at us with big, brown eyes glossy with tears and asked in broken English, "Do you think we make it? My belly hurts, and I scared."

Her older brother, Mario, wanted to ask questions also, but found it difficult. He asked, "How we eat for new day? No food almost?"

Daniel answered the eager kids through chattering teeth, while I snuggled under his arm in the warm seat next to him. We sat right behind

Mr. Mike's body and rubbed our hands in front of the bus heaters. Out of habit, I bent down and gently touched our driver's forehead. He was warm and breathing.

"You're going to be alright, Mr. Mike," I whispered. "You just hang in there. We tried to find help, but got too cold. We won't give up though. You told me I was a fighter, and I am, Mike. We need you to fight too."

Instinctively, Daniel put his arm around me, and Emily threw a warm thick blanket on me. She said while we were gone she and the others found a trunk of survival stuff. Mr. Mike had a hidden stash under his bus seat just in case of an emergency! They found it when she was rolling him over to prevent bed sores. That would've made me laugh, if I wasn't so grateful.

Emily was in the middle of reading off her new roster out of her notebook, but I was melting. The blanket warmed me to the core. All I could think about was food, warm food not stale food. I would eat anything.

Heated blankets were the best invention ever created, I thought. We were so glad to be back on the bus and out of the cold that it took me a few minutes to look for my brother.

"Where's Sammy?" I said, turning around to peer over bus seats. I assumed he moved towards the back of the bus to sleep, so he could watch for me out the back window.

"Um...ya'll oughta tell'er shouldn't ya?" the little girl they called Spare said, looking to Neova and Emily for answers.

"Sammy ain't here no more," Billy blurted out. "We ain't got no idea where he is, but he went and took off last night after ya. We woke up and he was done gone."

Neova cut him off, "We figured he would find you and Danny, and he would be with you when you got back."

"What?!" I said. "We didn't see him. We saw no one. We made it maybe two miles through the woods, and we saw NO ONE."

Suddenly, not even the heated blanket kept me warm. The reality my little brother wasn't here with the others, safely waiting on this warm bus, chilled me to the bone. So, where was he? I looked past Daniel out the window, as the snow continued to come down in white sheets. We hadn't seen Sammy at all on our trek through the snow. My poor baby brother was out there somewhere all by himself, probably freezing to death. I jumped back out of the pleather seat and moved back towards the bus door. Daniel grabbed my arm, pulling me back next to him in the seat.

"Let go! I have to go find him," I said, beginning to shiver in panic, swinging at Danny, trying to free my arm. Daniel didn't loosen his grip.

"You can't go back out there, Jett," Daniel said. "It's too cold. You have to get warm and get something to eat."

"I have to," I said, continuing to jerk my arm away from him. "I can't just leave him out there. He's all alone."

"How could you?" I said with a shockingly calm voice. My angry eyes pointed straight at Neova. "I asked you to do one little thing for me. I went to go find help for all of us and for you. And all I asked from you was you to watch Sammy."

They purposely kept from me the fact Sammy was gone, while I sat here comfortably relaxing. Neova wasn't the only one to blame. All of them kept it from me. They all tried to tell me their version of how they woke up, and Sammy was gone. They tried to say Sammy had opened the bus door without anyone hearing it and just left. I didn't believe it.

"Someone heard him leave! I know they did!" I said louder than I meant to.

"Yep, I heard someone leave," one of the little boys said. You could tell he was scared. "I didn't know who it were though. I thought maybe ya'll were back, and I was still asleepin'. I was 'a too cold to git up and look. Then when we all got up and around and saw he was missin' I felt real bad."

The boy's name was Billy. He had to have been telling the truth.

"I promise you, Jett," Neova said, reaching for my hand. "I didn't hear a thing, or else I would have stopped him."

Although I believed both of them, I was so scared, I put all of my frustration out on all of them.

"Everybody knew Daniel and I went out there to get help!" I said. "All I asked before I left was you all would watch over Sammy! How hard was it? How hard could it have been?"

I finished my last question before breaking down. I'd never been so scared in my life. Sammy was the only person who kept me going each day. I would have given up a long time ago, if I didn't have him. I knew I was the only one who would watch over him no matter what. And I had deserted him. He probably left, because he didn't believe that I'd come back. No one left and came back for me...or Sammy.

On the other hand, my history with Neova was too much to ignore. I couldn't trust she actually even watched Sammy or listened to him fall asleep before granting herself her own rest. She'd turned on me before. For all I knew, she'd told Sammy to go find me, just to put him in harm's way to get back at me.

I've snapped before, but never so quickly. I couldn't hold it in, and I knew why I directed my anger towards Neova. She'd put me through so much already with turning on me, tricking me into going to her apartment, cutting my hair, threatening me, and even beating me up. It had been a long time coming, and I was done bottling it all in. Neova may have had her friend Say to beat me up, but it was Neova with me. I had my chance to tell her finally what I thought. And now she had let my baby brother wander off into a frozen wilderness, and for all I knew he was freezing somewhere out there in the woods. He'd be lucky to make it an hour.

"Don't lie to me, Neova," I screamed, lurching towards her. I'd become someone else. I'd become a person who scared me. If I'd gotten a grip on her neck, I easily could've choked her. I'm not even sure if I would've regretted it in the end. In fact, I probably would've danced around her dead body, knowing what she did to me and now what she did to my brother.

"I didn't let him go anywhere," Neova said. Her voice was shaky. From all of the times she'd been to my house, she knew Sammy pretty well. "He snuck out while we were asleep. I have no idea why he'd take off like that."

"I asked you to do one thing for me, and you couldn't even do that," I said, overly articulate with anger. "You knew exactly what he planned to do. Come look for me. You thought it would be funny, if he froze to death, just like I did....looking for help...for the other kids ...and even for YOU!"

The more I spoke, the angrier I got to the point where my vision was blurry. I thought of nothing other than grabbing her throat and choking her.

What she said made sense, but it didn't matter. I needed someone to blame. My stomach hurt with fear for my brother.

"Neova, you are the last person I ever wanted to be stuck with in the middle on nowhere. I hate you, and what you did to me!"

My voice shrieked through the cold air, and the little kids got quiet. They were scared of what I became. Even though I felt sorry for them, it didn't stop me from continuing.

"How could you do such a horrible thing to me? We were supposed to be friends!" I yelled. My hands shook uncontrollably. I resisted the urge to grab her hair.

"Friends?!" Neova interrupted, standing in her bus seat. We had an audience, but it didn't matter to us. It had been a long time coming.

"Jett, you are the one who betrayed our friendship…you and your new friends."

"New friends?!" I said. "I have no friends now, thanks to you! There is no excuse for what you did to me. You are evil, and you aren't anything like I thought you were. That night you were like possessed."

No one moved as they listened to us scream at each other. Daniel sat there. He reached for my arm once, as I clenched my fist, ready to punch her in her nose.

Although I quickly tightened my knuckles, I hit her with the truth instead.

"I trusted you, and you turned on me!" I yelled. The quiet bus felt like a cold cave, echoing 'me…me…me…'

"I turned on you?" Neova repeated. "I thought we were friends, Jett. You were the first person who I thought really got me. But when we started school, you ignored me. I saw you with your new friends. What about what you did to me? Do you remember how many times you stood with your new friends, making fun of us? You joined in calling us names in the hallway, posting rude comments online. Oh, and you thought you were especially cool when you got a popular boyfriend. I went along with Say. Even though I shouldn't have, but I did it, because I was hurt too."

"But you went too far," I answered. My voice became muffled.

Realizing what Neova said was true, I knew deep down I ignored her on multiple occasions in the hallway. I walked right past her on the way to class, even when I heard her say my name. For once in my life, I was popular. I accepted Neova as collateral damage.

"I didn't really expect them to hurt you like that." Neova said, looking at my hair. Although it had somewhat grown out the colors had faded, my hair was still nothing like it was before. Neova's eyes seemed sincere.

"I may not have been the nicest person to you, but no one deserves what you and Say did to me," I added in a whisper. Neova stood silently, dropped her head, and started to cry.

"I'm sorry, Jett," she finally muttered in between sobs. "I hate myself for what we did."

"You should," I said. My angry, hostile tears became sad tears, as I relived the night.

Neova called me that day during our winter break. She asked, if I wanted to hang out. The call was surprising, since we hadn't spoken for a while. We'd drifted apart over the past few months. I had nothing else to do. I took the short walk from the trailer park to Neova's apartment complex. Something didn't feel right, but being naive as usual, I figured we would watch a classic movie like we did last summer and pretend we would be famous someday.

I planned to become a famous photographer and Neova planned to be a chic hairdresser to the stars. We planned to become roomies in a swanky high rise somewhere in the city. When I got to her apartment, Neova opened the door before I knocked.

Over her shoulder, Say reclined on the couch, watching TV. Say reminded me of a cat, lackadaisical one minute and pouncing unexpectedly the next.

"Come on in, Jett," Neova said, seeping with sappy enthusiasm.

"Yeah, queen of Jefferson Junior High, come on in," Say meowed from the couch.

Something didn't feel right. I nearly turned around and left, but Neova pulled me over to sit in front of the TV like our friendship had never faltered. The girls watched a historical account of Cleopatra.

"What a tough bitch," Say said, adoring the harsh tactics Cleopatra took to maintain power. "Poisoning your own brother? Cleopatra must've been cray-cray. I mean to the second power of crazy. Lovin' it."

After another fifteen minutes of awkward silence, watching Cleopatra's power dissolve into ruin, Say pounced.

"So, Jett, why did you choose to grace us with your presence today?" she slurred. "One of your status shouldn't be seen with our kind."

"Why, Say, you look as enchanting as usual," I responded. "I especially dig the black combat boots with striped socks, although I'm not sure if the look screams Tim Burton or reminds me of a witch crushed under a house."

Say started to answer, lifting herself from the couch.

"Now, girls," Neova said. "Can't you just get along for one hour? Nothing better to rekindle friendships than a makeover!"

Noeva and Say looked at each other, and Say nodded. At the time, I assumed Say was agreeing to play nice.

"I just got new make-up and a new curling iron I've been dying to try out," Neova said.

It wasn't the first time Neova used my perfect hair to practice for beauty school. She was amazing. Say followed us down the hallway into Neova's bedroom. I plopped onto the beanbag in front of the mirror as usual. Neova put her desk chair behind me, assembling her tools. Hair spray, hair glitter, hair brushes, and curling irons. Neova had it all. One of my favorite parts of Neova's makeovers was wearing my sleep mask, so the final outcome was a complete surprise. Ceremoniously, I released my long, blond hair from its ponytail and pulled my hot pink sleep mask over my eyes.

As I took a final glance into the mirror to mentally save the "before" image, I saw the two behind me. A cold chill rushed through me after seeing Say's smirk, but I dismissed the warning.

"So, where am I going?" I asked slowly, wondering why they both suddenly were so quiet. This, too, was part of our makeover ritual. Say describes the special event I am preparing to attend, and she tells me her plan of attack to make me beautiful. Still silence and no movement. I felt Neova's deep breath on the back of my neck.

"Hello? What will it be this time? An elegant up-do for the Oscars? Or long, wild tresses for a dance party?" I asked.

Just as I moved my hand up to my face to take off my mask, someone slapped my hands down.

"Now, Jett, patience." It was Say. "Rome wasn't built in a day, remember. Neova's going to have to work really hard to make you look good."

"Well, that was rude," I replied. I dropped my hands, assuming Neova would start on my hair any minute. Say grabbed my hands again. This time she held them together and locked them in handcuffs.

"What in the heck are you doing?" I said, feeling the tightness of the cuffs.

"Don't worry, Jett, you're getting a makeover all right," Say said. "I think you oughta try a Mohawk or something...um..not so boring. This long, blond hair is just a little too "cool girl" *cliché*." She emphasized *cliché*, and I knew she was mocking me.

"What? What are you doing now?" I asked. My voice transformed into a shrill shriek I no longer recognized. "Why'd you put me in these handcuffs?"

No one answered. I heard giggles. One girl whispered to another.

"Neova? Are you still here? I thought you were my friend?" I asked, with my question bordering begging. "This isn't funny. If you guys think you're playing a joke on me, it's not funny."

Neova didn't say a word the entire time. The giggle really didn't sound like hers, but, apparently, I didn't know her that well anyway.

"Oh, I'm pretty sure that it's going to be pretty funny," Say said to me.

"Do it. Come on. You can't chicken out now. We've gotta do this before your mom gets home," Say whispered. Apparently, she was convincing Neova to do something.

"Do what?" I asked, fighting the urge of becoming hysterical. I knew this was bad. I kicked at anything close to me, knocking over bottles of something.

"Hold still, princess," Say said. "We're starting your make-over."

Say held me down, while I felt something being poured onto my head.

"What is that?" I screamed. It was cold, and I recognized the ammonia smell. They were coloring my hair.

"No, guys, please, don't do this," I begged. If they were bleaching my hair, what else did they plan to do?

The cold liquid rolled down my forehead and a few drops made it through the mask into my eyes before I lifted my cuffed hands to block them. My eyes burned like an inferno. I screamed.

"Help! They're going to kill me! Help!" I screamed until one of them stuffed a dirty sock in my mouth. I choked on the raunchy taste and felt it settle in the back of my throat. Claustrophobic. Next, I heard the distinct sound of snipping scissors. It must have been Neova since Say was sitting on me.

"At least take the sock out of her mouth, so you don't suffocate her," Neova said. Her voice shook as she asked Say to stop. "I don't think we should do this."

"If you won't cut it, she will. She already put the color on like we planned," Say said.

There was another person in the room? I heard another person moving around, but she didn't speak.

"I'll take this sock out of your mouth, but you keep your mouth shut," Say said, pulling the nasty sock out.

I gagged again, spitting once she removed the sock.

"Why are you doing this?" I asked. None of this made sense.

"I said to keep your mouth shut, or I'll gag you with the sock again," Say answered.

Neova and the other person remained silent. I figured it was their other little follower. I didn't even know her name, but she followed them up and down the hallways at school.

"Neova, are you there?" I pleaded. "Why are you doing this?"

My scalp burned from the hair-dye. I imagined the mess they made with my hair. Someone grabbed my hair and started chopping recklessly with the scissors.

"What are you doing?" I screamed. Hair fell around me. I visualized a rainfall of hair all over me and the floor. "You're cutting my hair? This makes no sense."

"You know what makes no sense," Say said. I recognized her voice anywhere. "You. You make no sense."

Neova continued cutting my hair, while Say told me what a horrible person I was and that I should just go home and kill myself. At least I now knew she didn't plan to kill me. After another minute of verbal bantering and hair-cutting, one of them jerked my arms, forcing me to stand up. The handcuffs rubbed my wrists raw.

"Please stop," I continued to beg. "Where are you taking me?"

"I said to shut the hell up," Say said, "or we'll shut you up ourselves."

I chose to stay quiet, although I couldn't imagine what they planned to do to me next. One girl dragged me through the house by the arms, while the other slapped me several times in the back of the head.

"If I were you, I'd hit her harder," Say told her. I assumed it was Neova, since the other girl didn't have any reason to hate me. "Bring her in here and let's rinse out her hair. I can't wait to see what our beauty queen looks like now."

One of the girls pushed my head down into the tub, or what I assumed was a tub, while the other rinsed my hair out. I could taste hair color and gagged again. If they held me down much deeper, I'd drown. The tub's drain was clogged, and water began to rise. At one point, one of the girls shoved my head under water.

Pulling me out of the soapy water, gasping for air, I heard one of them yell through my clogged ears, "Maybe if you stop being such a snobby bitch, we won't kill you next time."

So, they planned to kill me. A scream escaped in a pitch unrecognizable even to myself. One of the girls slapped me across the face, knocking me back onto the bathroom floor.

"Please, don't kill me," I cried. "I'm sorry. I'm sorry."

"Now, you're sorry?" Say said. "You'll be really sorry when you look in the mirror, beauty queen."

And she laughed a laugh that would haunt me in my nightmares. The girls pulled me off of the bathroom floor by my short hair, or what was left of it, and led me down the hallway towards the living room. My mask was still intact, but I could tell where we were based on the sound of the television and the scratchy couch they pulled me past. Once we made it back across the small apartment to the front door, the girls opened the door and pushed me outside onto the ground.

I started to stand up to run away, when I felt the cold air blowing in from outside, but one of the girls pushed me back down onto the ground again. I heard two girls laugh. Another muffled voice in the background was indistinguishable. There were three girls, I remembered.

Another girl smacked me right across the face, while another girl kicked me several times. After several blows, I stopped asking them to stop. I kept my arms over my head, took the hits, and cried.

"Why are you doing this?" I asked repeatedly.

"Because you're trash!" one girl answered.

"Because we hate you and you should die!" another girl answered.

The girls used some sort of phone app or something to disguise their voices.

Their words were distorted into terrifying voices. The flurry of insults hit deep inside beyond my flesh and bones. I knew these bruises would never fade.

"That's enough," one of the girls, who sounded like Neova, finally said. "Let her go."

Someone jerked my wrists up and unlocked the handcuffs. My arms and wrists ached and were rubbed raw. She dropped me onto the cold concrete.

"Don't you dare tell anyone, or we'll find you and the next time, we'll keep your head underwater," one of the girls said still using the app to change her voice.

I was already drowning in fear and sadness for my baby brother, not to mention the rest of my crappy life in poverty. Remembering that night and what happened to me felt like someone holding my head underwater.

The entire time, though, Daniel held me, just like a good friend would, letting me fight my way back up to the surface for breath. I finally released everything I'd held in. The bathroom incident of smashing stuff the day before helped, but I had not fully let it all go. With Sammy missing, I couldn't take any more.

"God, if you're out there, I need you," I prayed, as I cried. I no longer cared who saw or heard me. It didn't matter. I didn't cry and pray to make Neova feel bad. I was sincere. It was a painful, from the gut cry that took everything from my heart.

"Please be with Sammy," I continued in my prayer. "I don't even care about what they did to me anymore! I just need you to be with him, please."

NEOVA

There was too much time to think. Amidst my thoughts were many regrets. I knew I should've stopped Say. She told me her plans, and I went right along with her. Say was my best friend, but I knew she was dangerous. The plan was to invite her over and snip some of her hair just a little to get back at her for ignoring me at school. Jett also said some pretty nasty things to the two of us at school, knowing they weren't true. She deserved what we planned to do, or that's what I told myself. When Jett got to my apartment, though, I already regretted it. What really bothered me when Jett went off on me earlier on the bus, though, was she acted like it was only me who did all of that. Maybe she didn't know there was a third person? It wasn't only Say and me at my apartment.

Surely, she heard all three of our voices. When they attacked Jett in the apartment, I was there and helped, but the other two did a lot more than me like the hitting, name-calling, and handcuffing. If I hadn't talked them into stopping, I'm afraid of what might have happened to Jett. Once they got started, the two girls flew out of control.

Asking Jett if she knew about the other girl would only bring back up the topic of that horrible night. With Sammy missing, Jett has been too distraught to talk to her about anything. Sleeping through Sammy's escape off of the bus was another regret on my mind. Jett had every right to hate me. Right before Sammy went to sleep, I wrapped a blanket around him and gave him his stuffed rabbit. Sammy asked about his sister.

"Do you think my sister is okay?" he asked me. His eyes were full of tears. "I sleep with her every night."

Sammy was such a cute kid. When Jett hung out with me, before school started, she often brought Sammy along. He was never any trouble. She doted on him, and he was so adorable you couldn't help but to baby him. If Sammy left in the middle of the night, that meant he had been in the snow for at least six hours.

Even though it was a little warmer than Friday, it was still frigid outside. I read a book one time about a little boy who got lost in the woods and survived because a wolf slept with him. The wolf's body heat kept the little boy warm through the night. Was that a book I read? Or was it *Jungle Book*? I couldn't look over at Jett again. Daniel sat with her, and her head was on his shoulder.

Chloe had been pretty quiet. I went to sit by her. If nothing else, it would pass the time.

"How much longer do you think we can wait?" I asked her. Less than one week ago, Chloe wouldn't have said a word to me at school. If she did, it would've been a bad word. After being trapped with me on the bus, she was far less likely to cast stones in my direction. Yesterday, she even complimented my handwriting. I'd written a letter to my mom just in case....I couldn't finish the sentence. I wanted to make sure she knew how much I loved her and appreciated everything she'd done for me.

"I'm not sure," she answered.

Of everyone, Chloe became the most negative and depressed on the bus. No one blamed her because of our circumstances, but it was such a different person than who I saw every day at school.

"You holding up?" I asked.

Chloe continued to stare out the window for several minutes. On the bus, there was no rush to answer anyone. We had nothing but time. I sat and watched out the window with her, giving her as long as she wanted to answer.

"Earlier, I stared outside so long my eyes burned. I forgot to blink," Chloe said. "The more I looked outside, the more I believed there was a fire truck driving down that hill to save us. When I blinked and looked again, it was just a cardinal."

Outside of the bus window at eye level, the cardinal sat, pecking at a red berry on a tree. Jett would have said it was a photo op, but I didn't point it out to Jett since she was trying to sleep. She hadn't even closed her eyes yet. A blue bird swooped down and landed next to the cardinal; the cardinal didn't even flinch. The two picked berries from the same branch.

"I get excited when a bird flies by the window," Chloe said. "Look at them. Isn't that cute?"

Her grimace didn't match her words.

"They are cute," I said. "Funny how the two are so different, but know how to co-exist. Even birds realize there should be no competition. Different isn't bad."

"You're right," Chloe finally said.

Her eyes never left the birds. I was worried that she couldn't handle this pressure. "They are very different," she added, "Both are just as beautiful as the other. This is the first time I've stopped to look at birds in a long time."

"Me too," I answered.

"I'd much rather the cardinal be a fire truck of course," Chloe said, pausing with a rare grin on her face.

CHLOE

For the last three nights and countless daytime naps, I awakened from the same nightmare. My mother tucked me in, like she had done Thursday night, the last night I saw her. Her lawyer voice transformed into baby gibberish.

"Chlo, chlo, who's a good girl? Chlo, chlo...." my mother cooed at me.

"I'm a good girl, mommy," I sang back to her in a little girl voice.

She kissed me good night. Then all of a sudden, my mom turned into a cardinal and flew away.

I was left alone in bed, repeating, "I'll be a good girl. I'll be a good girl."

I woke up crying, missing my mom and even my dad, as quiet as he was. I wished I had kissed her good-night, and I regretted refusing her a hug. The rest of my time on the bus was spent feeling bad about everything else I had said or done to my parents or to kids at school.

I was lethargic with guilt and fear of what was to become of all of us. No one was going to ever find us. They would have found us already, if they were going to, I thought. Throughout the last few days, there were different times we thought helicopters flew right over us, but we weren't sure if it really happened or if it was just wishful thinking. My sullen attitude transformed into self-despising.

Deep down, I knew although I wished I had treated my parents differently, there was more to my dark mood. Guilt sucked any ounce of joy out of your heart. I knew what I had to do. The timing wasn't the best, but it had to be done. We weren't guaranteed to make it another day on this bus.

"Jett, can I talk to you?" I asked her, looking over the bus seats.

Jett raised her head off of Daniel's shoulder and looked surprised.

"Do you need something?" she said. Jett wasn't going to be easy to convince to move to my seat.

"I wanted to ask you something," I answered nervously.

"Well, ask me then," she said. We hadn't spoken hardly at all on the bus, and I knew she was hurt by the way I treated her at school.

"I'd prefer if we could speak in my seat, if we could?" I asked, hoping she noticed my humility.

"I don't really care what you'd prefer," Jett said. Her face was swollen from crying.

"My brother is missing," she continued, "and I can't deal with any of your drama."

"Please," I said so quietly she barely could hear me. "I really need to tell you something."

Daniel whispered something into her ear. Jett rolled her eyes, and reluctantly stood up and sat next to me. She was perched at the very edge of my seat, and I could tell she didn't want to get any closer to me.

"What?" Jett asked. She glared at me. I saw Neova watching us curiously. It was difficult to have any private talks on the bus without the others hearing.

"I wanted to say I'm sorry," I began. "I treated you so badly at school."

"How nice of you to apologize on your death bed," she said nastily. "You want to clear your conscience in case you kick the bucket, huh?"

"You're right," I said.

Jett finally looked straight in my eyes.

"If we weren't sitting here today, I can't say I would've had the courage to apologize like I should have," I answered. "I've said horrible things to you, and I wanted to tell you I'm sorry."

Neova heard our conversation and rolled her eyes at me. I knew what she was thinking. She thought that I had nothing else to say, but I did have more to say to Jett.

I took a deep breath and started shaking. "I've done bad things I knew were wrong, and…"

"Okay, Chloe, I get the point," Jett started. "You were a crappy friend and dumped me when I needed you most. And, if that wasn't enough, you stole my boyfriend. It's over now. You can have Keagan. He obviously didn't really like me anyway. He's a jerk, so the two of you are the perfect couple."

"No, there's more," I started, "that I feel I should tell you."

"Well, spit it out. What could be worse than making my life every day at school miserable?" Jett asked.

"It was me, Jett," I said. The words were balled up so tightly in my gut that it physically hurt to pull them out.

"I was wrong for what I did to you," I spitted out. My voice shook and screeched at the same time, but it didn't matter. The words needed out of my gut. "I was there that night. I was the third girl. I hit you, cut your hair, colored it, and called you names. It was me and Say."

While I confessed my abominations, Jett's face contorted from disbelief to pain to fury.

"So, you knew all along what happened to me?" she asked. "Not only did you know, but it was your fault?! You were supposed to be my best friend."

"I-I-I was jealous of you and Keagan, which sounds stupid now, but, at the time, I was sick with jealousy," I tried to explain. "I've liked him forever and thought this would be the year he would take interest in me. Then you moved into our school and stole my friends, my popularity, and the boy of my dreams."

"I thought you hated Say, and Say hated you?" Jett asked. "Why would she help you do anything?"

"We both had one common interest," I said painfully. "At the time, we both hated you."

"Oh, I see, you were supposedly jealous and hated me," Jett began, "until we nearly died in a bus wreck. You changed your mind when you saw me nearly freeze to death and watched me mourn the loss of my baby brother. That seems fair."

Jett's voice raised an octave before she finished. I felt like dirt. No, I felt like less than dirt. I felt like the maggots that wallowed in dirt on dead matter. Jett would never forgive me, and I didn't blame her.

"Your jealousy was no excuse for what you all did to me," she continued. "Chloe, you are a selfish brat. That's what you are a spoiled, selfish brat, who always has gotten her way, and if she doesn't she does what she has to do to get her way. You need to realize the world doesn't revolve around you."

I shuddered. She was right. If I didn't get my way, I took it out on everyone else. Jett's voice suddenly mellowed from anger to sadness.

She continued, "Do you know how badly you hurt me? I'll never be the same."

"Jett, you are so right," I answered. "I am a horrible person. I can't even believe what I've done, and I deserve to die of starvation or freeze to death. I deserve it, but I didn't want to die without being honest with you....and with myself."

Jett didn't answer. Neova's head was down away from me, but I knew she listened.

"I think I partly realized how selfish I was because I saw how selfless you are," I continued. "I've watched how you've treated me the past few days despite how I wronged you. You have been so nice to me, despite how I treated you at school. You volunteered to go look for help for all of us. Even if you hate how I treated you, you did all of this for me. I am sorry, Jett. I was a bad, terrible person. I am sorry."

I finished by breaking down. I hit my head on the bus seat in front of me. I fought the urge to repeatedly bang my head into the seat. At first, she didn't answer, and I didn't expect her to.

"I deserve to die here, but you don't, Jett," I said while weeping. "None of you do."

Mario, one of the little boys on the bus, who rarely spoke, began to cry. He said, "No more. Enough. No more. Enough."

Neova tried to console him. We needed to stop all of this. Who knew how much longer we would be stuck together, and we needed to keep peace in the meantime.

Finally, Jett spoke to me, "Chloe, I trusted you, and I thought you were my friend, but I was wrong. You're much weaker than I thought. I'm not letting you or the nasty things you said about me make me hate myself anymore. I love who I am, no matter what my hair looks like. Do you even realize I almost swallowed a dozen pills to kill myself? That's how low you brought me!"

By the end of her statement, Jett was standing over me. She clenched her fists, much like she had done with Neova. I waited for her to punch me in the nose. I wished she had.

"You know what though," Jett finished. "You couldn't have made me feel that low without me giving you power. So, that was on me. You no longer have any power over me. I don't care what you think."

When Jett finished her statement, I broke down and cried again, but it was more of a sad quiet cry. I put my head down into my lap with arms over my head. It was painful to hurt, and to know it was your fault that you were hurting so deeply and others had to suffer as well.

"I was wrong, Jett," I repeated several times, as I sobbed into my arms.

I didn't want to raise my face to look at anyone. I was too ashamed. No one said a word. Someone turned the bus engine back on, and heat began to blow out of the vents. Everyone was too hungry and too tired to expend any more energy on the argument we were having.

After several minutes, Jett finally answered my apology.

"Yes, you were wrong," she answered in a softer voice. I felt her put her hand on my back and her arms wrapped around me. "Chloe, I forgive you. It's hard because of what you've done, but I made mistakes too. I put my dream of becoming popular above everything. It didn't matter to me who I hurt. Even though I didn't destroy someone's hair or hit anybody, I might as well have. None of that matters to me anymore. Without Sammy here, this all sounds so silly."

"So, you forgive me?" I asked.

My hardened shell cracked. All of the fake mean girl faces, thoughts, actions fell out onto the floor, while I cried. I'd never be the same, which was a good thing.

Jett got up, moved down the aisle to Neova's seat, and sat down with her.

Jett said something to her quietly. I barely heard, but deciphered the words *I* and *sorry*.

TUESDAY

JETT

Monday had emotionally drained me. When I awoke the following day, I assumed the following day would be just as depressing. We followed our morning routine, as we had the last several mornings. We each got a baby wipe, one teaspoon of toothpaste, and small cup of water. We took turns going behind the trash bag to pee in the bucket or outside, if we needed to.

The best part of waking up, though, was noticing how bright the sun was. It was blinding through the bus windows. Icicles melted, looking more like waterfalls than stalactites. Daniel read my mind.

"Looks like we'll be heading back out again today," he said, staring out the window. "If it's warmer, we'll be able to move faster and get somewhere."

For the first time in days, I actually felt hopeful.

That was, until I remembered Sammy was gone. I couldn't even speak the words, but the fear Daniel and I would come across his little, lifeless body almost kept me from going out to search again. On the other hand, I told myself, there was a chance we could find him before it was too late. This motivated me to get moving as quickly as possible.

"Let's go," I said, hopping out of the seat. "We're not stopping until we find someone."

EMILY

Reviewing my table of food and supplies, I realized how dire our situation was becoming. Daniel and Jett said they were going back out again to look for help. I proposed we all go, since it was warming up, but they thought just the two of them could move faster. They were correct in their assumption, so I agreed to stay behind. To be honest, I'd offered to go along, because the bus was beginning to close in on me. There were only so many times I could complete a crossword puzzle or rewrite my notes.

Another issue of its own was the noise on the bus. Often it was quiet, but the smaller kids were loud at times, and they were beginning to smell like dead fish. The compromise was we all would get off the bus and walk a few circles around the bus. Although the fact the exercise would burn Calories, which we all needed to reserve, some fresh air sounded good to me.

When we decided to go outside, the little kids cheered, as if we were taking a field trip to a carnival.

So, thus, Daniel and Jett packed their backpack again with far less food this time and promised to return with help this time. I led a march around the bus with Chloe and Neova falling at the back of the line. We pretended to be soldiers marching off to battle.

I counted my steps as we walked around and around and around. The snow was melting, so the ground became mush and mud. By the time we made it around the bus for the fourth time, all of our legs and shoes were covered with mud from stomping.

Of all of us, it was me who started the whole mud fight. I couldn't resist. I stopped marching, bent over, and slung a handful of mud right at Chloe.

The pile of mud that looked like feces hit Chloe right in the cheek.

Everyone stopped.

"She done did it now," Billy said, laughing and pointing at my face. "Emily sure is smart to do such a dumb thing to Chloe. That girl's as mean as a snake. I wish I woulda though to throw it at 'er."

We all expected Chloe to turn crazy on me. I figured Chloe would yell or cry. Or curse at me. Or do anything except what she did.

Chloe bent over dramatically, picked up two hands full of mud and threw one at me and one at Billy.

Before the wreck, being dirty would have caused a nervous breakdown for me. Today, it didn't matter. We had fun. Everybody started to sling mud. We flopped in the mud like pigs making muddy snow angels. The little kids especially enjoyed this activity. I was the only one thinking ahead on how we would all get clean again, but I stopped myself. It didn't matter. I wasn't caring one bit about what I looked like or what anybody else was thinking about me. We were all kids, and we were having fun.

NEOVA

After playing in the mud, we all stopped to look at each other. Now what did we plan to do? It's not like we had a shower. I turned to Emily.

"Did you have a plan for cleaning up?" I asked. Emily routinely planned ahead.

"Nope," she answered. Everyone looked at her shocked.

"You ain't got no way for us to get all this here mud off us?" Billy asked.

He wasn't really much dirtier than he usually was on the bus. The poor kid lived in a trailer smaller than our bus. If he didn't have the backpack of food, we may have starved by now.

"Nope," Emily answered again. "I forced myself not to plan, and live in the moment. I am embracing Carpe Diem."

"You're gonna eat carp? Isn't that a fish?" Billy said.

"No Carpe Diem, the phrase coined by Horace in his ancient writings of Ores in 23 B.C.," Emily began. "The actual entire phrase in Latin was 'carpe diem, quam minimum credula postero,' which meant to 'sieze the day, put very little trust in tomorrow.' I've planned everything my entire life, and I chose to be in the moment, so to speak."

"How do you know all of that?" Chloe asked.

Chloe's normally perfect hair was smoothed down with mud. She didn't even care what she looked like for once.

"I went through a phase during which I was fascinated with ancient Roman literature, but I grew distracted with astronomy and moved away from the Latin writings," Emily answered.

"Wow," Chloe answered. We all waited for a sarcastic, rude remark.

Much to our surprise, Chloe continued, "You know what, Emily, you are so smart. You know like everything there is to know. I wish I was that smart."

"Well, I like the sound of that—Carpe Diem," I repeated.

Right as we started boarding the bus, muddy clothes and all, we heard a roar pass over the bus.

A helicopter flew overhead. We all jumped up and down, but we couldn't tell if they saw us. We no longer allowed ourselves the thought of being saved. Too many false hopes already crushed our dreams.

BILLY

I'm gonna go ahead and plan to stay on this bus fer a long time. We done been here for tons of days. The bigger kids been fightin' and holler' about stuff like boys and bein' bad friends and other stuff. I just wanted to yell at 'em that we're all starvin' and don't wanna hear 'bout none of that blasted BS.

We still ain't seen hide 'nor hair of Sammy. We're all sure worried 'bout him. He's a tough little booger though, so I bet he ain't doin' nothin' but sittin' around eatin' donuts in a fancy restaurant with his mama. I still don't get why he took off like that. Just the other day I was a tellin' Sammy 'bout Scruffy, my dog, who ran away on me. Scruffy wasn't really too cute, but he was a good dog. He had two different colored eyes and enough fleas to start a circus. I tole Sammy how sad we all were when one day Scruffy just up and took off out of the blue.

Sammy tole me something about becomin' a hero or a superhero or somethin' and how he'd find Scruffy for me when he got help.

Spare and me cried and cried all day 'waitin' for Scruffy to come back. He never did come back. I tole Sammy all about this, so I can't figure why he'd take off on all of us like that.

He tole me he missed his sister, but I ain't sure he thought about how cold it was gonna be out there. What I forgot to tell Sammy was that 'ole Scruffy came back to us one day. He just showed up at one of our neighbor's trailers out of the blue. I'm prayin' Sammy shows up just like that. I kinda doubt he'll show back up though, 'cause it's way colder and snowier than it was when Scruffy ran away.

With too much worryin' and cryin', we decided to get out and have a good'ole time in mud. It was still purty cold out, but we didn't care a bit. We all went around and around the bus like the horse ride at the fair. Then next thing we knew we all were athrowin' mud and snow. We were yellin' like banchee injuns. Today was the best day since we wrecked. I just wished Sammy coulda stayed on the bus and gotta throw mud with us.

When we were playin' and yellin', we were so loud that we almost didn't even hear them comin'. Out of nowhere, there they were just like we woke up from a bad dream.

A chopper swooped right over our heads, and we jumped up and down hollerin' at 'em. The chopper sent a big wind at us, and mud flung off my face a little. It figured these cops showed up just as we started havin' fun. I didn't really care too much though. Mario grabbed me and pointed up to the top of the mountain. I squinted to see what he was getting' so darned excited about.

Way up there—on top of the mountain—there were a bunch of people and police cars and other stuff I couldn't see too good.

I ain't never smiled so hard in my life. My face hurt like I'd been slapped I smiled so much and so hard. We were agoin' home!

CHLOE

I actually had one ounce of hope that things were better regardless of our current conditions on the bus. I went back to gazing out the window, feeling even if they didn't find us, I would die happy knowing I made peace with Jett. My cardinal sat perched on a branch outside of my window until a loud noise scared him away.

Another mirage appeared behind the glass window. I imagined so many by this point that I didn't allow myself to grow excited. This mirage looked more realistic than the last three hundred times I had seen it.

There was a faint blur of people in the distance. I wondered what kind of creatures this mirage would clear up to be. They glided across the snow as if it wasn't slowing them down a bit. The imaginary people moved towards us as if something was wrong and dangerous. They were probably just a few rabbits or some other type of rodent.

This mirage was the most realistic one yet, as the people were getting closer, and my mind wouldn't allow me to see what was actually there. This was it. I knew these visions weren't healthy for me, and now I officially must have lost my mind.

I decided I needed to have someone else see the creatures for what they truly were. Billy was the closest one to me. I told Billy I needed help and at first he didn't sound like he really wanted to help me. I couldn't blame him because the only time I talked to him was to say something rude or argue with him.

"Billy, what are those creatures moving towards us so quickly?" I asked, beginning to consider trying to hunt for food.

"You talkin ta me?" Billy said with shocking surprise.

He glanced out the window and exclaimed with great excitement that those creatures moving towards us were....

MRS. POWELL

My television stayed on day and night while I slept on the couch, waking every few hours to check my phone. Still no word. I couldn't turn it off for fear of missing a breaking news report. When I awoke first thing in the morning, I filled my cup of coffee and turned the volume up to hear what Miss Fancy Pants had to say.

Here at Channel 9 we have closely followed this story for the past three days, as the Jefferson Police Department continues their search for a missing school bus. Police Chief Donover will hold a press conference any minute now. Chief Donover told us there is a big development in this search. But, first a word from our sponsors.

Were they kidding? Who cuts off to commercial break when it's a huge news story? The following two minutes and thirty seconds was the longest wait of my life. Laundry detergent commercials and previews for the next *Dr. Z Autopsy Reports* episode were of no importance to me. All I wanted to know was what the police found. The news report returned with the police chief standing behind a podium in front of the camera. He spoke calmly into a microphone, but it was apparent he was shook up and hadn't slept for days.

Good afternoon. My name is Chief Donover, and I have been leading the search efforts to locate the eleven students who were on the missing bus with Mr. Mike Powell when the bus disappeared last Friday. We had several leads come in over the past two days, which led us to the bus this morning. All eleven children have been accounted for, safe, and alive.

We located the missing bus at 11 a.m. this morning down in a wooded culvert. According to the children on the bus, the bus slid off of the highway during Friday's snow storm. Students also reported once the bus was brought to a halt,

> resting on a guardrail, a vehicle struck the rear of the bus, sending it down the mountainside.
>
> The children reported they survived by eating food from one of the student's free food backpack given to him as part of a school program. Students also reported finding a survival kit from their driver, Mr. Mike Powell, that allowed them to eat for the past two days.
>
> Students will be able to share more details of their stories once they have been reunited with their families....um... and take a bath.
>
> We have one suspect in custody this afternoon who allegedly was guilty of the hit and run accident that caused the bus to break through the guardrail. The woman will be charged with driving while intoxicated, leaving the scene of an accident, interfering with a police investigation, and tampering with evidence.
>
> Many of you already know this, but besides being the lead investigator in this case, I also have a personal vested interest in its outcome. You see, my son, Daniel, was on that bus."

Chief Donover got choked up. He looked away from the camera and wiped his eyes. My doorbell rang. I was afraid I wouldn't be able to hear the television, but I had to answer the door. Hesitantly, I turned the knob, knowing it may not be good news on the other side. I knew what it meant to have someone show up at your door after an accident had occurred.

A police officer waited patiently for me to open the door. I said a quick prayer that he was here to take me to see Mike, and that he was alive and well like all the children. Thank God, Mike was in the hospital, and was alive. They wanted to tell me before it was announced on the news. When the officer left, I heard Chief Donover's final statement.

> Like many of you, this has been the longest four days of my life. We are so blessed to inform all of you that our children are all safe and alive. As soon as we have notified all parents, we will release the students' names. Thank you to everyone who helped lead us to our children.

The crowd of reporters and parents cheered when he was finished. I didn't waste any more time sitting and listening. The officer told me Mike was taken to the hospital with a head injury. Apparently, the children kept him hydrated throughout the weekend, and even moved him often, so he wouldn't get bed sores. Tears erupted in my eyes.

These children were amazing. Doctors told police Mike should make a full recovery, because those children were so attentive to his needs. I threw on the nearest outfit I could find to get to the hospital as quickly as possible. I almost didn't even change from my night clothes at all I was in such a hurry. My little car couldn't get me there fast enough. My arms ached to wrap my arms around Mike again.

I wasn't ready to let him go yet, and I planned to tell him all about it...every day for now on.

CHLOE

If I'd known we would be on television, I never would have participated in that dumb mud fight. That was my luck though. The first time I let my guard down, news reporters were waving microphones in my face. It was pretty funny though, because when the police found us, they thought we all had been dirty and muddy the entire time we were missing. They all kept saying what it a miracle it was we survived the wreck, even if we did get covered in mud.

The police told us they thought Mr. Mike would make it. He was especially lucky Emily knew how to treat him until he was taken to the hospital. I told her good job, and I surprised her by hugging her.

It was a brief, awkward hug, but we both knew we were connected for life. Looking around at Jett, Neova, the little kids, and Daniel, I realized how blessed we were to have survived. I spent most of the time on the bus, staring out the window for help and feeling guilt pump through my blood like poison. I was given a second chance for some reason, and I planned to do my best to not make the same mistakes again.

It was funny to me how once we all stopped watching for help, we were found. As we were loaded in a four wheel drive truck to drive to the hospital to have full physicals, I watched out the window one last time.

A cardinal landed on the little berry tree next to the bus again. He looked right at me. He had to be my bird—my cardinal.

I whispered to the bird, as if he heard me through the glass window, "Thank you."

I couldn't wait to see my mom and dad.

JETT

The bus looked lifeless, as we pulled away. The police divided us into two groups and transported us up the mountain. Our parents waited for us at the top. We all were overjoyed, but I couldn't feel anything really. All I thought about was Sammy. I didn't want to make it to the top of the mountain to face the world without him. I tried to ask the officers about my brother, but they all were so busy taking our names and information and checking to see if we were healthy that I couldn't get an answer out of him.

How would I tell Merl about Sammy.

The first face I saw when we pulled up over the hill back onto the road was Gwen. Her silvery hair shined like a light house. Next to her stood Merl and Sammy.

Wait.

Was that *Sammy*?

As soon as the truck was in park, I threw my door open and ran to him.

"Sammy!" I cried and lifted him into the air. "Where did you go? How are you here?"

"I walked," Sammy said. Merl grabbed me and hugged me next.

"Gwen found him," Merl explained through sobs. "Jett, I'm so glad you're okay. I've been praying for days. Thank God you're okay."

"What do you mean Gwen found him?" I asked confused.

"Well, honey, I don't drive much, but my car does still run," Gwen said, grabbing me for the next round of hugs.

"Yes, but where did you find him?" I asked.

"I was worried about you all, so I drove back and forth from the school to our trailers all Sunday and Monday," Gwen started. "It was after dark Sunday night, and I really shouldn't have been driving. Don't tell them officers, but I'm not supposed to drive in the dark. Anyway, I was driving along and singing to my favorite Dolly Parton song when there he was—the little angel was walking down the street with RaRa like he was taking a stroll in the park."

"I don't understand," I answered. "That doesn't make sense. How did he get all of the way up the mountain?"

We all looked down at Sammy.

Merl said, "We've asked him a million times, and all he says is the man carried him and dropped him off."

"What man?" I asked Sammy.

"I don't know, sis," he said. "I just wanted you after you left to get help, so I left the bus to walk with you. I was getting really cold, so I sat down with Ra Ra."

"And?" I asked.

"And I fell asleep and that man carried me," Sammy answered straight faced. He was serious. It still didn't make any sense.

"I don't know what else. I just walked for a minute, and then Gwen pulled up in her car," Sammy said. He acted like it all was no big deal. "I was sure glad to get home, but I've still been missing you. I had to sleep with Merl to get any sleep."

I wanted to pinch myself to see if Sammy was really with me, or if I was dreaming and would wake up on the bus again at any minute. It was too hard to believe my baby brother made his way all of the way up the mountainside to the highway in the middle of the night.

"Hey, Sammy, I missed you so much," I began.

We were all still crying tears of happiness. Merl, Gwen, and I took turns hugging each other, and then hugging Sammy again. Sammy turned so serious when I asked him about how he was found.

"Sammy, me and Daniel went out to find help, and we couldn't make it up the big hill, so we tried to walk all of the way around," I said and paused to hear his response.

Sammy looked back and forth from Merl to me with his eyes wide open.

"I don't know, sis," he said. "I can't remember a whole lot about it. I grabbed my blanket and RaRa and went out to find you. I thought I'd catch up and we'd find help together."

"I know, bubby," I answered. I didn't want Sammy to think he did anything wrong. How was Sammy found? We all needed to know, even though we were grateful beyond words.

"We're just trying to understand who this man was. You know, the man who brought you up the hill," I explained. Sammy nodded.

The tears evaporated in his eyes, so I continued, "This man must have been a hero, and we want to find him to tell him how happy we are he found you."

Sammy nodded and answered, "I tried to sleep in the bus after you left, but you said I could've been like Hercules. I wanted to show you how tough I was, and I didn't like sleeping without you. After a while of not finding you, I got really tired."

I interrupted, "So, you fell asleep in the snow?"

"Yeah, I think so," he said in his adorable voice. "I don't remember, but I think I fell asleep and woke up when he was carrying me up the hill."

"Who was carrying you?" Merl asked. She was obviously as perplexed as I was about Sammy's story. Throughout the conversation, Gwen stood next to Merl wiping her eyes and hugging her thick, faux fur coat around her.

"It was the man," Sammy said again. "You know, Mrs. Gwen's friend."

Gwen became wide-eyed at Sammy's admission, and she asked, "My friend? Sammy, who is my friend?"

He answered, "The man. The man who carried me and told me to shhhh....be quiet...she'll be along soon."

We all stared at Sammy in disbelief. He still held RaRa in his arms, while he answered our questions with pinched eyebrows, as if he focused as closely as he could to recall the events of two nights ago.

"That's what the nice man said," Sammy continued. "I was really cold, but when he picked me up and carried me, I got warm. He told me to sleep if I wanted to and somebody'd drive by and pick me up soon. At first, I was kinda scared because you tell me not to talk to strangers, but since he was Gwen's friend, I didn't think I'd get in trouble."

"Sammy, baby, are you sure you didn't just dream this?" I asked. I believed him wholeheartedly, but I had to ask.

"No," he said hesitantly. "I don't think so. He sure seemed to be real when he carried me."

"Who was he? And how did you know he was one of Gwen's friends?" I asked him. None of this made sense.

"I knew he was Mrs. Gwen's friend 'cause she had a picture of him at her house. Remember, sis, when we took Mrs. Gwen cookies for Christmas. We saw the man in the picture next to the Christmas tree. Remember? We left cookies and went back home. You told Mrs. Gwen we had more cookies to deliver, and we really didn't. I asked you why you lied to Mrs. Gwen when you're always telling me to be honest.

You told me Mrs. Gwen is like a grandma to us, and I said yes, she sure is. You said you wondered if the picture was her husband, and I didn't know what you were talking about, so I kept walking along with you until we got home. Remember? The picture of the smiling man with blue eyes in the blue shirt next to the tree? It was him. He wore a jacket not a blue shirt, but it was the same man. I promise it was him."

Sammy looked from me to Merl to Gwen, as he described the man who he claimed carried him up the mountainside. Immediately, I wondered if Sammy could have invented a story like this, but he had never been known to tell stories. And, if he did make the story up, how did he walk all of the way up that mountainside by himself and so quickly. It took Daniel and me hours upon hours to walk in the thick snow on flat land.

Gwen stared at the melted snow on the ground, throughout Sammy's explanation. Merl cried in disbelief, as he recalled how he was saved. Merl didn't know about the picture at Gwen's house, but she felt the magnitude of the miracle anyway.

"We believe you, but it's hard to grasp," I said, trying to get more details from him. "Try to remember really hard everything you can and tell us."

"When I woke up, we were at the top next to the road," Sammy said. "The smiling man said he had to be getting back, and some nice lady would be along soon for me. Um, I remember I asked him if he was an angel."

"What did he say?" I asked. This entire story was so hard to believe, but Sammy gave us so many details.

"He said he wasn't like an angel, but he wanted to help me like a guardian angel," Sammy recalled. "I just about asked him where his wings were, but he kept talking to me. The man said he was helping the nice lady out 'cause she watched over all of us, kids, and he couldn't imagine what she would do if something happened to us. He said he loved that nice woman a whole bunch and to tell her that he'd see her again soon. That's just about all I remember, because I was so tired."

Merl pointed at Gwen's car parked on the side of the road. The police had the road blocked, so everyone could park and leave despite the dangerous curvy road.

"So, this is where you picked Sammy up, right?" Merl asked Gwen.

Gwen wiped her eyes before looking up at all three of us and replied, "Yes, this is where I found him. He didn't know where the bus was, so I couldn't tell police when I got back home and called them. I was able to give them some idea of where I picked him up though. I barely knew where we were myself, because it was sleeting so hard, and I don't see very good at night."

"You believe me, don't you, Mrs. Gwen," Sammy asked, looking at her. "I'm sorry if I made you sad."

"No, honey, you didn't make Mrs. Gwen sad," she answered him. "Actually, you made me happy...very happy. I've been wondering about him lately. I miss him."

"So, he was your friend," Sammy said. "Sis, we should make him cookies next time too, since he helped me."

Gwen watched the flurry of activity around us, appearing to decide how to respond.

"I don't think you can, sweetheart, he must have moved on by now," she said. "You see, that was my husband."

"Your husband?" Sammy answered.

"I think you may have met my husband," she said again with more certainty. "He had to go on a trip, so it will be a while before I see him again, but I am sure glad he helped you out."

Before allowing herself to give in to her emotions, Gwen changed the subject, "This old car has racked up more miles in the last week than it has in the last ten years." She climbed into her car, and invited us all to get in as well. "I'll take you, Jett, to get checked out, so you don't have to ride in the ambulance."

"Oh, great, thanks," I answered, turning one last time to check on everybody else. We all looked a mess. Since Daniel and didn't get too far on our second journey for help, we saw the police when they arrived at the bus. We both died laughing when we noticed the rest of the kids were all covered in mud.

Chloe was hugging her parents. The three of them held each other and cried.

I heard Chloe's mother tell her, "Everything's going to change, ChloChlo. Me......and daddy are going to be here for you. We aren't going to let you down."

Billy and his sister, Spare, stood next to their dad and stepmom, who I recognized them from the trailer park. Mario and his family huddled together as well. We all made it.

Unbelieveable. I took the lens cover off of my camera and started clicking the scene in front of me. National television station reporters stood behind a thick rope denied access by the police. I wondered if we were on television? Maybe I could see if any of them wanted to see my pictures? I definitely had a front row seat in this story.

Daniel stood next to his father, who faced the rest of the parents with his arm around his son. When he saw me looking at him, he winked.

I walked over to tell him goodbye, and he stepped away from his dad.

"I told you he wouldn't give up," Daniel said with an adorable grin.

"He's not the one who technically found us," I teased him, "but you were right. He didn't give up."

"Well, I'm glad we got to know each other," he said, becoming nervous all of a sudden.

"Yeah, me too," I answered. Daniel had to be able to hear my heart pounding through my chest. He looked around at everyone around us absorbed in their own conversations, and looked directly at me.

"I meant it when I said you're beautiful, Jett," Daniel said quietly. "You don't need to worry about what your hair looks like or what anyone else thinks. You're beautiful because you're kind and brave."

Daniel was so serious. The two of us had nearly died together, but now we were thrown so quickly back into reality. We weren't sure how to act around each other.

"Thanks, Daniel," I said shyly. "You're pretty swell yourself."

"I'll see you on the bus when we go back to school?" he asked. "Or can I call you?"

"You can call me," I said, grinning from ear to ear. "I don't plan to ride the bus again for a long time."

"You're right," he said, laughing. "Me either."

Neova stood nearby with her family as well wrapping in a huge heating blanket. Chloe and Emily both were sharing their experiences with their families. Last week, I would have rather poked my eyeballs out with a fork than be around those girls. I walked over and hugged each one of them, including Emily.

We all had a deeper understanding of each other than I ever imagined we would. It was hard leaving them behind. I turned and got into the car with Gwen. Merl and Sammy followed us in our car.

"I can't even wait to hear about the adventure you just had," Gwen said, as I snapped my seatbelt.

"You'll never believe it," I said.

"I think it's time you and me start over again," she said, as I climbed in. "We were so scared of losing you and Sammy and the other kids. I know I had a lot of time to think."

"What do you mean?" I asked confused.

"Well, I've been cooping this old body up in my little trailer, living with a bunch of dolls and cats who can't even talk to me," she began. "I think it's time I moved."

"No, Gwen," I said. "You can't. What would we do without you there watching us?"

"Well, I think I'll still be around to watch the kids, but I spoke to your mother, and she finally gave me permission," she began.

"What? You don't have to have my mom's permission to move out," I answered. Her words scared me. "Where are you going? We just made it back, and you're going to leave us?"

"No, Jett, what I mean is, *we're* going to move," she began. "*We*, as in you, Sammy, and your mom, are going to move.

"We?" I asked. None of this made any sense. "The four of us are going to move in together?"

"I already spoke to your mother about all of this," Gwen explained. "There's a nice, big house not too far from Todd's for sale, and I think we should go take a look at it. I told your mom I would take care of you and Sammy, while she worked."

"What? Are you kidding me?" I asked. "That would be amazing! A real house?"

"Yes, a real house, and it has a pool," Gwen said. "I just happen to have a little money put away I need to spend."

Gwen drove down the snow-covered road like a turtle down the road, or I would have hugged her. Instead I grabbed her arm and squeezed it, careful not to jerk the steering wheel. Her brightly colored nails matched her eye shadow. Only Gwen would get this made up to find lost children.

"Thank you, Gwen!" I said. "And not just for the house. For being here for me, you know."

"Oh, sweetheart, I needed you as much as you needed me," she replied. "You came along at just the perfect time. I was just about to give up and let all of those dusty dolls cave in on this old lady."

The image of Gwen covered in dolls forced me to smile again.

"You can't just throw them all away when we move," I answered.

"Oh, I couldn't do that," Gwen said. "My stomach hurts thinking about it, but I will have to find a place to store them out of sight. The realtor said the house has a full basement and five bedrooms."

"Five bedrooms?" I gasped. The only house I'd ever been to that big was Chloe's, and it was like a mansion to me.

"Yes, little lady, and a full basement for you and your friends to hang out," she answered, stealing a look at me. "Hanging out is what you all call it these days, right?"

I didn't answer. I didn't have any friends. Neova and I made up, but I didn't know, if I could ever trust Chloe again. But there was Daniel, I remembered.

"We may even use some of that money I've got put away for a big TV," Gwen said. Her eyes shined with excitement, and she looked much younger than when I first met her.

"I definitely can't keep all of my cats either," Gwen continued, more to herself than to me. "Well, we'll figure that all out later. For now, be careful or we'll end up down the side of that mountain again."

"No way," I growled and let go of her soft arm, momentarily recalling the ordeal of the last few days. The horror was washed away with the excitement of a new beginning. This called for picture-taking, so I clicked away on my camera, documenting every angle of Gwen's face and hands with the snow falling behind her.

"Oh, my, gosh, this is the best day of my life," I squealed. "I'm warm and get to eat...and get a new home!"

"Yes, little girl, you do, and you deserve it," she said, nearly accelerating above twenty-miles-per-hour. "Once this snow all melts I'm going to have to go buy me a hot pink swimming suit for that pool."

We both laughed, and I added, "Maybe I'll have hair again by then."

"Oh, Lordy, we can only pray," Gwen said.

The two of us laughed until we cried all of the way to the hospital.

CPSIA information can be obtained
at www.ICGtesting.com
Printed in the USA
FFOW01n0915201015
17848FF